By Any Other

Name

By

AJ Brewster

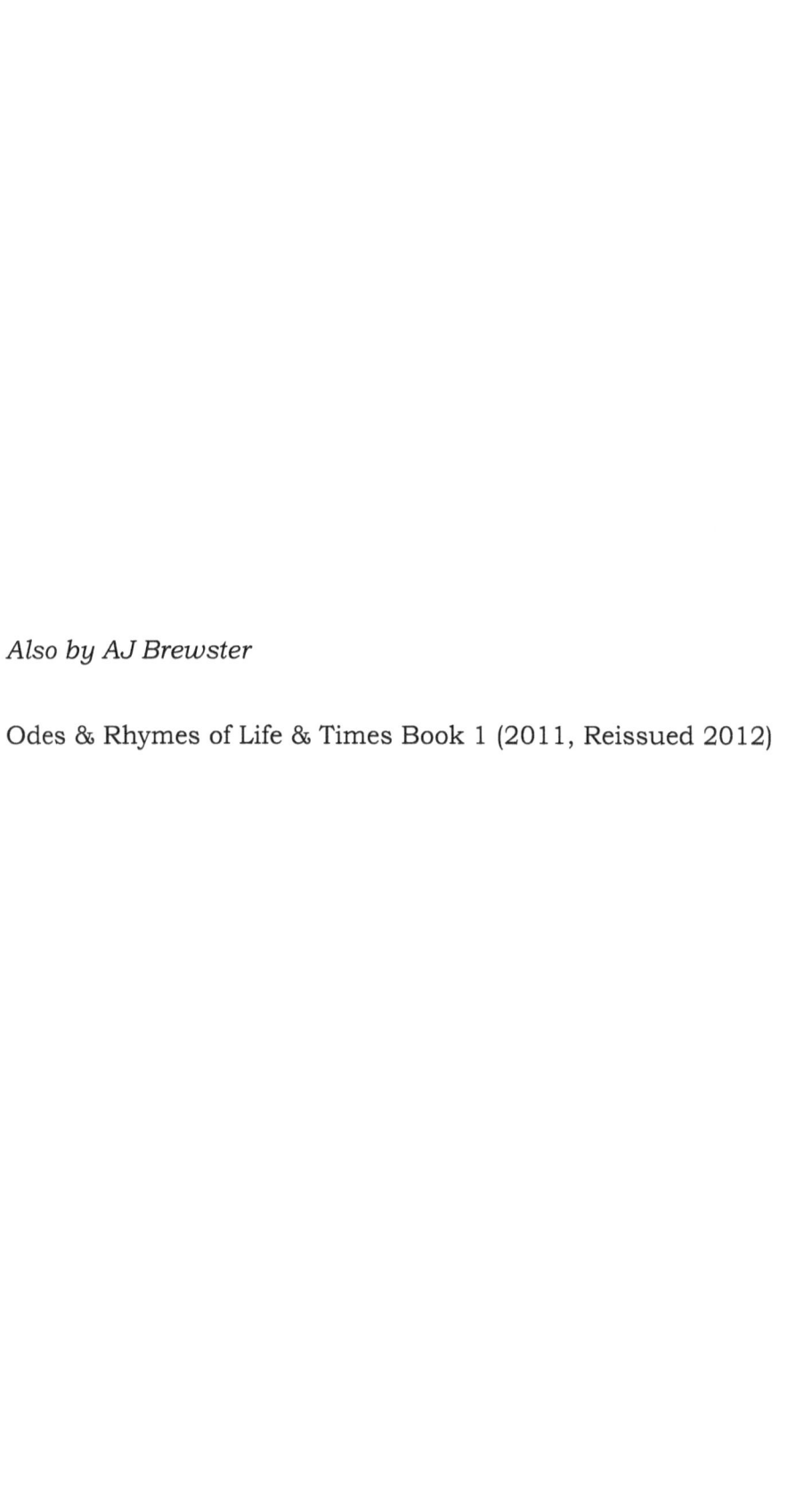

Also by AJ Brewster

Odes & Rhymes of Life & Times Book 1 (2011, Reissued 2012)

I can't begin to thank all my friends and family who have stood by me and shown me so much support over the years with my writing and my website, www.thetwistedtalesofajbrewster.com.

So, in no particular order, a special thanks to:

Lee Daly, Garry & Becky, Jenny & Trevor, Conor Daly, Debbie & Ian, Sandy & Dave, Bev & Kev, Ian & Helen, Lee & Di, Janet, Wendy & Paul, Muriel Eade, Lucy Drury, Rachel Mercer, Nichola Churchill, Sam Bossley, Rebecca Wildman, Linda & John, Sharon & Ian, Trina & Neil, Carlene Wade, Kim & Mark, Clare Johnson-Smith, Debbie Clarke, Ellie Jones, Karen Palmer, Jane Morris, Anne Dale, Julie Clarke, Simon Mullins, Stuart Wood, Darren Lafon-Anthony, Stewart Lenton, David Sandbrook, Ricky Collins, Andreas Rohregger, Tatiana Salazar, Lee Cooper, The Burton Family, Jean Coleman, Kirsten de Savary, Sally Booth, all at Profile Tree, Annie Hatcher & Blyth Powers Ashes attendees, Libby & The Barge Long Eaton and, of course, my wonderful Grandparents.

If I have missed you off my list and you bought my previous book of poetry 'Odes & Rhymes of Life & Times', I'll apologise in advance now and promise that if you review both books on Amazon and you'll definitely get a mention in my next book. Cheers AJ

Prologue

December 1st 1986

Rose carefully closed the door to the tiny one bedroom flat so as not to make a noise and disturb the baby or wake up her boyfriend, fearing her boyfriend more. Her nose screwed up involuntarily as she was met by the smell of rising damp, B.O. and stale alcohol. It always smelt stronger when she returned home from her work as an office cleaner and she could clean all day and never remove the damp smell.

Rose knew that the situation she was in was her own doing but she wished more with each passing day that she had listened to her father's words of warning when she had first taken her boyfriend to meet her parents. Maybe if Rose hadn't of been so stubborn then she wouldn't be in this dreadful predicament. Her parents had only met him once but that was enough for her father to make his mind up and, despite her protests, stubbornness meant that he would never change his mind. Rose guessed that was where she had inherited her stubborn streak from. There wasn't a single day that went by when Rose's thoughts didn't linger back to that day, regretfully going over the 'what ifs' in her mind and wishing she'd have listened to her father's words of discouragement.

September 29th 1984

The day had started out so well, Rose's nervousness seemed needless as her mum welcomed them into the family sitting room for afternoon tea and cakes. Rose had always known that her boyfriend's way of life would never meet up with her father's requirements but as they sat on the sofa she grew more hopeful that if her mother could see how much they loved each other then, with her help, Rose would be able to persuade her father to see it too. With that little twinkle of expectation, Rose had decided it was time to take him to meet them.

They'd sat there as her mother poured out the tea using the best china while explaining that father would be late as he was seeing to the gardener because the green fly were in the roses again. It was very pleasing to the eye with the colourful Fondant Fancies, Battenburg and butterfly cakes adorning the three tiered cake stand that was also part of the matching best china. Mother, enjoying the company of romantic young love as she would devour up every word of a Mill's and Boon romance that you would always find her reading, was asking questions about how they met and where they'd go out of an evening. Sighing and cooing at every special thing. It was as if the romance had been missing from her life for so long that she needed to be reminded of every little detail. Everything was so polite and relaxed until her father walked in the room with his matter-of-fact attitude bringing everyone down to Earth with a hard, bone-crunching landing.

From the minute her father walked through the door, the atmosphere became heavy and the whole room seemed to grow smaller adding an element of claustrophobia to what was to become a seriously strained situation. Rose's father sat down in the armchair across from them, arms folded and brow furrowed. The same look that had been used when, as a child, Rose had picked his prize begonias and used them to practice pressing flowers as homework from school. Then came the torturous bombardment of questions to her boyfriend and the answers to which were always followed by accusations and derogatory remarks. Every so often her mother would say, "Now, now father, I'm sure it's not that bad." And she would smile awkwardly at them both knowing deep down that no one would change her father's views on the subject.

No lies were told but in this case lies would probably have been the better option. Once her father knew his background he wouldn't stop dictating, letting him know that without a shadow of doubt he would never be the man for his daughter, that his daughter was destined for great things. She was going to Oxford University for God's sake. And Rose most certainly did not need a man like him. Then it was her turn...

"How could you choose a man with no class? You could be with any of the most promising young men at our parties, so why choose this low life over one of those?" Her father chastised. "It's not just the fact that he's grown up in the wrong area. He has no money and with his job, how do you expect him to fit into our society. Plus, his father is a permanent resident of Her Majesty! It rubs off you know! That's if it isn't already in his blood!" And so it went on with his last words being said as they walked out the door to the car, "It won't work! You mark my words if you marry him *then you will be divorced in a year!"*

And it was those words that it had stuck in her head nibbling away at her whenever things were going wrong and just lately they had gone very wrong. It wasn't because of his council estate upbringing, not because of his employment or social skills and not because his father was in prison but because of her father's stubborn lack of understanding and because of Rose's rebellious nature she had stayed with him all this time trying to make it work and trying to prove her father wrong. Rose did a very good job at it too! She fell pregnant within a few months of moving in together and had to leave university early. Thinking that it may help if her parents knew that they were going to become grandparents, she went over to tell them the good news. On hearing the news her father disowned her and forbade her mother from seeing her. And now, still afraid to contact them, she lived the life that she had made for herself, one of misery and abuse.

It was dark in the room but she could sense angry eyes staring at her, cutting into her like a sharp knife, drawing her life's essence out of her, weakening her until she felt she could take no more.

Suddenly the table lamp came to life. Rose blinked for a few seconds allowing her eyes to become accustomed to the blinding yellowish glare of the bulb through the creamy dust covered lampshade.

"Where have you been?" Her boyfriend yelled, his eyes cutting into her like scalpel trying to dissect information rather than flesh and bones. Scrutinising her, trying to find answers in her facial expressions, her mannerisms.

Rose has grown to know that he didn't really care where she'd been or what she'd been up to. By the bottles that lay around the room, empty of the contents that had so cleverly convinced him that his insecurities were real and had driven him into yet another wildly jealous rage, Rose knew that he was just trying to find some information that he could use to pick a fight, and then it would end up how it always ended up.

It started with a good drinking session followed by his imagination running riot with pictures and information collected from pure fantasy. More beer would follow to help contain these pictures, adding more kindling to the jealous rage that grew like a wildfire inside. Finally the beer was replaced with whisky or some other spirit and this would convince him that everything he had been imagining was actually a true event, so this then led to the uncontrollable anger that was eventually dampened by a session of beatings and brutal sex, which would then convince him that he had control of the relationship but more importantly control of her. Why couldn't he be normal and make-love like they used to do? It seemed like they always had to fight first so that he could feel in control and powerful.

He seemed to enjoy hearing her cry and scream. He liked to slap her and punch her. Belittle her. For some reason these things excited him. He enjoyed seeing her in pain, enjoyed hearing her plead. It never used to be like this. He used to be so romantic and Rose used to love him so much but now, well, the romance wasn't there and neither was the love. Rose hated him. She hated him so much that if she had the strength Rose knew she would kill him.

When it first started the neighbours would call the police. The police would come and then go after being told the situation was all right. Now the neighbours didn't bother anymore. She was on her own.

"Where have you been?" He yelled again, waking her from her thoughts.

"I...I g...got h..held up. We...we had a very busy night. I had a lot of cleaning up to do. The office had an after work party and we had to wait for them to finish and then clean up the mess." She stammered nervously, praying that he'd believe her and not cotton on to her plans.

"You're lying." He shouted and jumped up from the armchair knocking the nearly empty bottle of Jack Daniels to the floor. Rose jumped too and began frantically looking for some way to get past him to the bathroom so she could lock herself in and escape his torture. "Tell me the truth you slut. Where have you been?"

Rose, alerted to baby John beginning to cry because he had been woken by the noise, knew that the bathroom was no longer an option and she headed for the bedroom door to make sure he was okay. She'd only just made it to the door when a hand swung round, hitting her on the side of the face and knocking her to the ground.

Rose lay there dazed, her head spinning while her face became hot with the stinging sensation that his hand had left behind. It took her a few minutes to realise what had happened but by then it was too late to do anything about it. He was already on top of her, shoving her skirt up, tearing at her tights, pushing her knickers to one side and thrusting himself inside her, his anger transforming to pleasure as he did so.

"Get off me!" Rose screamed, summoning her strength to try and push him off and even though she knew it was useless, she knew she had to try. "Leave me alone!" Pushing hopelessly against his huge, bulky body, Rose's strength started to fade. "Just get off me and leave me alone!"

The more Rose said that she didn't want it, the more he was enjoying it, thrusting harder and harder. It was becoming more painful with every thrust. Sending shooting pains into her stomach and making her feel sick. Rose could still hear John crying in the bedroom, even above his grunting and her whimpering. She wanted to go to him but knew she was going nowhere until her boyfriend had finished with her.

Rose tried to remember the good times, tried to switch off to what was happening. Tried to remember how he used to take her to fancy restaurants, tell her how beautiful she was and buy her flowers to cheer her up. How he had been so happy when he first saw his new born baby son. It was like someone had taken the man she loved and replaced him with this workaholic, alcoholic bully. He still bought her flowers but they were only to say sorry for what he'd done. At first she believed that he was truly sorry convincing herself that he hadn't meant to hurt her but now she took it for what it was, a ritual that he couldn't live without. He would never change and she couldn't stop him from being the animal he was. Rose drifted into a mind-numbing stasis, entering a protective world where she left her body and watched from above, allowing herself to be used as he willed.

Then with one terrifyingly violent thrust it was over and leaving her in a weakened, jelly-like heap on the floor he went into the bathroom, slamming the door behind him.

Rose returned to full conscious and got up as quickly as she could, ignoring the searing pain between her legs, trembling, she hurried into the bedroom. Sobbing, she picked up John and holding him close to her, she whispered in his ear.

"You are the only good thing that's come out of this relationship. After tomorrow there'll be no need to cry anymore. Don't worry, we're going somewhere nice, somewhere he can't hurt us anymore. We'll be rid of him tomorrow."

Rose sat on the edge of the bed rocking back and forth, feeling at ease, hugging John like a child would hold its favourite bear after being woken by a nightmare. Inhaling the baby's relaxing scent of talcum powder and E45 cream, that always made her feel calm. As if sensing that everything was going to be all right, John stopped crying and went back to sleep.

Rose put the sleeping child back into its cot, staring at him for a few minutes and then changing into her pajamas. She climbed into bed, positioning herself as close to the edge as she could without falling out and pulling the covers round her neck, leaving her torn blood stained clothes on the floor to deal with tomorrow.

She lay there sobbing for most of the night not daring to go to sleep. Waiting for him to come in from the bathroom and climb into bed beside her. Sometimes he would do this and it would all start again, like bell starts the next round of a boxing match, something would go off in his mind and the commentator would yell "Round two".

Sometimes he would come to bed and go straight into a heavy sleep and Rose would lay there listening to him snore, relieved that the nightmare was over for another night.

But on this occasions Rose's boyfriend didn't come to bed. She didn't really know what happened, he probably sat in his armchair continuing to drink until he eventually fell asleep. Of that Rose was very thankful.

When Rose got up in the morning he'd already gone off to work. She'd heard him come into the bedroom for his work clothes and had pretended to be asleep to avoid any further confrontations. Looking at the clock, Rose could see that she had four hours to get packed and make her escape before he came back for lunch. She didn't own much so it wouldn't take very long but it didn't stop her from feeling nervous. What if he came home early and caught her packing? She had to take that risk and began the task while John lay on his play mat with his teething ring firmly gripped in his hand and gums.

Rose had been right it hadn't taken more than an hour to pack every meager item she owned and with John sound asleep in his Moses cot, she began to wish she'd said an earlier time for collection. Rose sat in silence sat staring at the clock, listening to it tick away while she willed the hands to move a bit quicker. Hoping that she wouldn't hear keys in the door before the car horn sounded to indicate that it was time to go. Rose jumped when finally the sound of the horn peeping it little getaway SOS broke the only sound that she had been listening to for the last half hour, but just to be sure Rose held her breath and went over to the window just to double check that it was for her.

On seeing the friendly red car, Rose sighed and waved to

indicate the coast was clear then she grabbed all her bags taking them outside, coming back for the baby while the car was being loaded up.

Rose had met Karen through work and as they cleaned the office building together they had become very close. Karen didn't get on with her family either so she and Rose had a lot in common.

Karen had become more concerned with each fresh bruise that appeared. At first Rose had lied about how she'd got them and Karen, being a friend, pretended to believe her but eventually Karen got the truth out of Rose and it was Karen who had finally talked Rose into leaving and moving away with her, convincing her that she couldn't stay there and bring up John with that monster around. Between the two of them they could afford to live and bring up the child.

It had taken a while to get a place and a job sorted, all the mail going to Karen's so that Rose could keep it all a secret, knowing too well what would happen if her boyfriend ever found out. The last pieces of the puzzle were put together last night as Karen and Rose stayed late at their cleaning job to plan her escape.

As Rose climbed into the passenger seat of the 'get-away' vehicle she felt the tears make tracks down her cheeks as the sense of relief overwhelmed her. She took one last look at the dismal place that had been her prison for the past two years, and then closed the door on her nightmare to start afresh with a new name in a new town.

When Rose's boyfriend returned home everything seemed a little bit too quiet. It was unusual to not hear John crying or playing as he came to the door. He unlocked the door and stepping in, he called, "Rosie, I'm home."

No reply.

"Come on Rosie, I'm sorry. I've brought you your favorite flowers."

No reply.

He threw the flowers on the sofa and strode into the bedroom.

"Rosie!"

No one in the bedroom.

"Rosie!"

No one in the bathroom.

She must have gone down the shop for something for his lunch. He was just about to go and make himself a cup of tea when went off in his brain. He ran back into the bedroom, he hadn't noticed straight off that John's cot was missing. Looking in the wardrobe, he noticed her clothes were gone too.

He could feel the anger welling up inside him and slammed the wardrobe door which immediately broke from its hinges in protest at the brutality. "I'll get you back for this Rosie. I'll get you back, you'll see."

Chapter One

September 13th 1987

He only had to look at the outside of the house to know that it was just what he wanted it. Maybe it was slightly run down but he could make it into a lovely place for his Rosie to live in when she came back to him. Besides it was all he could afford while he kept up the rent on his flat in town until it was liveable. It was sad that his Grandparents had both died in that house fire but with all the charity shop clothes that he had grown up wearing they could have saved a bit more money, taken out some life cover or something. After all the effort he'd gone to, covering his tracks by making sure that the fire looked like an accident. He'd done such a good job of it and his acting was worthy of an Oscar when he was told of his

Grandparent's 'unfortunate accident'. All that effort to be left a measly ten grand after funeral costs. It's a shame the charity shops didn't sell second hand coffins they certainly would have been a lot cheaper and would have reflected his Grandparents life perfectly.

Rosie had been gone for nearly a year now but he hadn't stopped looking, or given up hope. He knew as soon as he found her she'd come back to him and if she didn't, he'd make her. Of course he'd have to make sure that she didn't leave him again. The Estate agent said something, waking him up from his thoughts. "I'm sorry." He said, "What did you say?"

"Are you sure you don't want to look around the house sir?" Jeremy, the man from the estate agents, repeated unsure why any man would want to buy a semi-derelict house without looking inside. Jeremy came to the conclusion that maybe he wanted to buy it, renovate it and sell it at a profit. Everyone that Jeremy had shown round before had looked around inside and that was what put them off buying it. It was just too much work. Mind you this man didn't look the type to have the kind of money to shop around. His jeans were ripped, his t-shirt was hanging out and his trainers were so worn that it would be a certain bet there were holes in the soles. He smelt like he had been out on an all-nighter with the lads and didn't have time for a shower before his appointment. In fact his whole appearance was very scruffy but then builders usually were, and he did have the muscles for a builder. With a makeover and a bath, Jeremy thought, I could really go for those muscles.

His dark hair hung in longish waves, which if cut shorter would have been the curls of a dark-haired Adonis. He was very tall and unshaven but it all added up to a very rugged look, definitely not the type with money but who was he to argue, he didn't care so long as he sold the house.

"No, I can see it's perfect for what I want it for." He said smiling.

"Oh, so you *are* looking to renovate, well this is a perfect property for that. I knew from the minute you walked into the office that you were a builder looking for a profitable project." Jeremy said, grinning with a smugness that could only match Kenneth Williams in one of his many Carry On performances.

The man just smiled at him and looked at the house once more. Its windows and doors were boarded up and some of the bricks looked about to crumble but it was cheap and there was a telephone box directly across the road, so he wouldn't have to get a phone line put in. It was a fairly quiet street made up of about ten detached houses. All of the houses were empty and had 'For Sale' boards up apart from a couple which were right down the other end of road and looking at those you would think they were empty too. It was perfect.

Jeremy couldn't believe his luck. Ever since he'd been working at Mason Collins Estate Agents this house had been for sale. It was a right mess, full of damp and mushroom-like mould. Some old lady, too old to do all the jobs that were needed had lived and died in there. It was such a secluded area that the old lady hadn't been discovered for about three and half months. She wasn't too pretty when they found her from what he'd been told. There was a rumour that she had been murdered but there was not enough evidence to warrant an investigation. Apparently, the estate agents had tried to clean it up a bit but his boss had told him that there was no way to clean up the smell of death and that the only way to get rid of it was to pull it down. Their only hope to sell it would be someone willing to put an awful lot of time and money into it.

Jeremy couldn't believe that, at last, it was actually going to be bought, and that he would be the one who would sell it. The boss was going to be so pleased. Maybe he'd get a large bonus for finally getting rid of it. He would definitely be out on the town tonight to celebrate. Maybe he'd check out that new club that all his friends were raving about.

"If you're ready we can go back to the office and get the paperwork started?" Jeremy suggested eager to close the deal, just in case the guy changed his mind.

Rhonda screamed, struggling to escape the man's vice-like grip. She wished that she had checked out this client a bit better before she'd agreed to meet up with him for sex but he'd paid upfront for tonight and it was not a measly sum of money either. Double her normal rate and he'd offered it to her without asking her for her rate first so she accepted before he had the chance to do so. 'Beggars couldn't be choosers,' as they say.

When Rhonda pulled up outside his house in the taxi however, she had some reservations about the decision she'd made and was just about to tell the taxi driver to take her back, thinking that perhaps she'd got the wrong address, when she noticed that he was already in the front garden smiling at her. Taken in by how charming he'd looked, she forgot about her reservations and jumped out of the taxi, thinking that the house's outside appearance wasn't too bad and maybe it was better inside. She'd never been good with the warning lights in her head. Tended to ignore them, then get into trouble and this was just another one of those times.

He'd been okay when they'd first started, just a lonely guy talking about how his wife had taken the kid left him and how he'd just wanted to feel close to a woman again. He seemed like he wanted to talk more than have sex and Rhonda began to feel at ease but knowing her job was to please him sexually she'd tried to oblige him with a more meaningful sexual experience. They'd been at it for ages now and quite frankly she had run out of ideas to get him turned him on.

Maybe if she hadn't suggested that she'd give him a refund minus the taxi fares because he didn't seem to be attracted to her, she'd be all right now. It was up until that point that he'd remained calm, even though he couldn't get it up. Now he was like a maniac, wanting to slap her, scratch her, and bite her. It was then she said that she didn't do violent sex games and he'd dialled the wrong number if that was what he'd expected to get for his money but she could introduce him to some girls that did if he'd wanted her to. Rhonda tried so hard to be accommodating to his needs but the more she protested the more he pushed. It was when Rhonda got up off the bed and started to dress so she could leave that he grabbed her and forced her to the floor.

Rhonda kept struggling and eventually his hold loosened a bit, allowing her to bite his arm and pull herself free. Using the edge of the bed as an aid, she stood up and as he grabbed her leg to pull her down again, she grabbed a lampshade from the bedside table and struck him over the head with it. It didn't knock him out but it gave him something to think about, which in turn gave her the time she needed to grab her stuff. Pulling on her fake fur coat and grabbing her white stiletto shoes she ran downstairs. She ran as fast as she could through the part-restored house and out into the back yard, only stopping at the door to put her shoes on before leaving. She could hear him cursing as he came running after her. Rhonda looked around her quickly, taking in her surroundings. On noticing the telephone box, Rhonda reached for handbag and realised that she had left her bag back in the house. Now her only chance of escape was to run up the road and knock on some of the doors to get attention. She turned and ran out of the garden and up the street. To Rhonda, the houses didn't look lived in but there had to be someone around. There was a light on the porch of one of the houses at the other end of the road so someone must live there.

Rhonda could hear his footsteps getting louder. She risked a glance behind her and could just about make out his shadow; he was gaining on her fast. It was like a bad dream, she ran faster but never seemed to get closer to the house while the bad guy seemingly gained ground behind. She had to lose him. There wasn't enough time to make it to the house at the end of the road. Turning into the yard of one of the other houses, she ran round the back and ducked down behind a crumbling coalbunker.

From behind the coalbunker she could see into the kitchen window. Worn unit doors were hanging open, some only by one hinge, exposing the inside of a dusty but empty cupboard. She could hear his footsteps coming up the path. Rhonda watched him as he first tried the door to the house, and then began looking round the yard. She had to make a run for it if she didn't it would only be a matter of time before he found her. Rhonda held her breath as she watched him walk towards the coalbunker. Her heart was pounding so hard that she felt sure the noise was going to give away her hiding place. He started walking over towards the coalbunker. Rhonda couldn't decide whether to carry on hiding or jump up and try to fight her way out of the garden. Suddenly there was a sound over the other side of the garden, his head turned to look where the noise had come from and as she followed where he was looking Rhonda noticed a shed further down the yard. The door was moving ever so slightly in the wind. Rhonda watched as he walked towards the shed muttering, 'Come out, come out, wherever you are'. Watching his hand reach for the door handle Rhonda realised that this was her chance and she readied herself to run again. As he opened the door and entered the shed, she stood up and ran. In her haste to escape she knocked over an old terracotta pot and alerted him to her presence.

Rhonda heard him swear and begin to run after her. His footsteps were a lot heavier than hers. Feeling like he was directly behind her, breathing down her neck, Rhonda carried on running fighting the urge to look behind her in case he *was* that close.

Oh God, she thought, please don't let him catch me. I know I haven't exactly been a saint but I have to make a living somehow. Please don't let him hurt me.

As Rhonda came out from beside the house on to the road, she didn't notice the brick that lay in her path, and tripped up, falling flat on her face. She could feel the blood trickling out of her nose from where she had struck the edge of the path. That was the least of her worries she had to get away. As she tried to get up, a pain shot through her ankle. She tried to scream for help but even her voice box betrayed her as nothing more than a pitiful whimper managed its way past her lips.

Giving up, she grabbed the cheap, tacky crucifix now fashionably worn by Madonna that hung round her neck and began to pray for the first time since leaving the Private Catholic Girls School that her parents had sent her to.

As he came closer, emerging out of the shadows, she saw him pull a knife out of his coat pocket. As he held it up high, ready to plunge it down into her chest, the blade caught the light given off by the large full moon. It was about six inches long with a white stone in the handle.

"No...Oh God no!" She screamed. The blade plunged through the air, seemingly in slow motion. She felt it impact with her chest. It's sharp, cutting pain as it went in. It's slow, dragging pain as it was pulled slowly out again. Her mouth filled with blood. The metallic tasting fluid blocked her windpipe as she tried to breath.

Suddenly she heard the sound of a moped in the distance and as the noise came closer he jumped up and ran and hid. The moped pulled up beside her.

"Are you OK lady?" A man's voice asked then noticing the blood he yelled, "Oh my God! Stay with me, I just need to nip home and call an ambulance and I'll be back. I won't be long."

"Don't leave me..." Rhonda said and started to choke on blood but the man had started his moped and didn't hear her pleas. He shot off down the road.

Coming out of hiding he didn't stab her again. Instead, she felt him use the tip of the blade like a pen carving shapes carefully across her stomach. He then slashed at the side of her neck, sucking and licking at the wound, gorging himself as a vampire would do in a Hammer Horror movie.

He obviously thought that she was dead because he got up and walked away. Rhonda tried to move, tried to drag herself down the pathway. If she could just make it to the house with the light on, which the moped was now parked up outside of. With every stretch of her arm she could feel the nerves surrounding the wounds send a sharp reminder of their severity.

She hadn't gotten very far when he returned and dropped something beside her. She tried to turn her head to see what was so important that he had to return but by then the world had started to spin and turn black.

Detective Harris looked at the map of Ipswich that lay before him. Putting his hands to his head, he massaged his temples trying to relieve the headache that hammered like he had seven dwarfs hard at work inside.

All the murders had taken place in the Rosehill area of Ipswich. For the murderer to be able to disappear without a trace he either had to live in that area, or he had to know Ipswich well enough to be able to get away and hide quickly. He could have a car but there were no skid marks near the scene of any of the bodies and no one had heard any vehicles leaving in a hurry. The other conclusion to this was that he had time and that thought scared Harris more than anything.

Harris looked at the pictures pinned to his wall. This maniac had to be caught. He had pictures of the girls before and after the murders. All the girls were very attractive, with long, straight, dark-brown hair. They were all of average build, slim with curves in all the right places. That was the problem. The only thing that they had in common was their looks. Their ages, lifestyles, jobs were all very different, very different indeed.

The first had been at Rosehill School on Derby Road. A young teacher, she had been teaching a late adult ladies class on self-defence. It was as she was leaving the building to go to her car that the murder must have taken place. Initially, when Harris had turned up at the scene, he'd been informed that it was a failed robbery and thought it to be true until he'd noticed the keys still clutched in her hand. Looking at the way she had been holding them, she had tried to use them to defend herself against her attacker. Sadly all she had managed to do was tear the assailant's clothes before being knocked unconscious. When the autopsy had been carried out, they then found out that she had been raped. She was one of the less mutilated bodies and the attacker had taken the time to put her joggers back on, which showed the possibility of remorse for his actions. She was only twenty-six years old, single and still living with her ageing mother.

The second had been only a short distance from the first. Her body was found in the churchyard where Rose Hill Road crossed Alan Road. They believed her body had been dumped there as her husband had said that she'd always insisted on getting the bus back home so that he could leave their toddler in bed. She worked late nights at a service station and the graveyard was neither close to her place of work, the bus stops or her home.

She was thirty-nine and was pregnant with their second baby. Again, the victim had been re-dressed after the rape had taken place.

After that things escalated out of control with any remorse the killer had felt for his victims going rapidly out of the window. The third was found on Rose Hill Crescent, she was aged between twenty-five and thirty-five and had no identification on her. They would have assumed a robbery if the killer hadn't left his calling cards. From the state of her hands it was clear that she had put up a fight with her assailant and that this had made him angry enough to destroy her face. They still had no identification on her as yet. They were hoping to identify her by matching her teeth to dental records but until they got a match she would remain unknown.

It was the forth that had disturbed Harris more than anything. The girl had only been eighteen years old. She worked part-time as a waitress for a busy restaurant in town and had been walking to work when she was murdered. When she didn't turn up for her evening shift her boss became worried and called her parents, who then called the police. That was the only way they knew who she was because like victim number three all personal possessions had been taken. Her body was just about identifiable by her father. Harris had then watched as the father's composure crumbled at the sight of his daughter's mutilated body. Apparently, she had just received her acceptance letter for Cambridge University in the post that morning. She had her whole life before her.

The style of the murders, however, had plenty of connections to point to the fact that they had been carried out by the same individual. All the victims had been raped and had a crisscrossed knife wound to the neck. The murderer seemed to have an obsession with roses because he had taken the time to use a knife to carve 'Rose' into the victim's abdomen. All the victims were found with a white rosebud beside them. All the victims were found in or around the Rosehill area and he would take the time to drop off the body in that area if murder wasn't carried out there. Even the sites where they had been found had rose in the name or were situated near a road or place with rose in the name.

The profile report from the psychologist suggested he was aged thirty to forty-five, very insecure with a need to be loved and a deep hatred of being rejected. Outwardly he would give the appearance of being happy-go-lucky, while underneath the surface he would be quite angry and confused. It's possible that he experienced or witnessed beatings and/or sexual abuse as a child and probably found it hard to enjoy sex normally but would find it extremely pleasurable when violence was introduced as his strong desire for complete control over his victims was how he got satisfaction. As a child he would have made the connection between violence and affection from an early age and this now meant each time he committed a crime he would have to take it one step further to be satisfied completely.

Harris had taken extra precautions this time. He had placed police all around the Rosehill area. Posters had been put up to alert everyone in the neighbourhood to be vigilant and to call the police if they witnessed anything or anyone out of the ordinary. He was going to catch this maniac, even if it killed him trying to do so.

He threw his plastic cup at the bin on the other side of the room. He missed. "Story of my life." He said to himself. Glumly, he got up out of his chair and walked over to the bin. Picking up the plastic cup, he placed it carefully in the bin and walked slowly over to the window.

As he stared out into the night sky, lights glittered in the surrounding buildings like stars would have lit up the night sky had he have been in the country instead of the town. He wondered whether the killer was out there tonight, lurking in the shadows of the town, watching, waiting for his next victim to walk past him, unaware of the imminent danger hiding around the next corner. It had been nearly a month since his last murder. Would he kill again? Deep down Harris knew he would. The murderer was an obsessive and that meant, until he was caught, the killing would become more frequent, the period of time between them would diminish but this obsession would hopefully be his downfall. Would they ever catch him? Well that was the question that was troubling him more than anything.

Chapter Two

Emma moaned as she awoke to the sound of the workmen on the street outside. It was only nine-thirty and she had wanted to sleep in until at least eleven this morning. Why did they have to ruin it and start work today of all days? She had wanted to sleep in late because she started her new job at the bar tonight. Laying there, trying to block out the noise with the pillow wrapped around her head didn't work, so she decided it was better to get up than lay in bed wasting the day away.

It still felt strange to wake up in her new home. Even though she had her best friend Jackie just a couple of streets away, she just couldn't get used to living on her own but Emma knew that with all the arguing at her parent's house she just had to move out. Living alone was better than playing 'Piggy-in-the-middle' with her parents. Forever being asked to take sides; who did she love more, her father or her mother? It was always a constant stream of bickering, picking, poking and general slagging off.

Anyway, to cut a long story short, for Emma's twenty-fourth birthday her mother, trying to buy her affections, had given Emma a thousand pounds. Then, trying to beat her, she'd received two thousand pounds off her father. Emma took the money, put it with some of her own that she'd saved and said, "adios amigos!" Then heading into town, she went and put a deposit down on a mortgage to get this place. It was a bargain of a place. Two bed-roomed Victorian mid-terraced house with a separate dining room and thankfully an upstairs bathroom. It had a small walled garden out back which meant no big lawns to take care of. It was just right for the modern, single girl about town. Plus it also meant that if she did meet someone special then she didn't have to embarrassingly explain that she still lived with her mum and dad.

Emma rolled to the side of the bed, sticking one foot out from under the edge of the duvet to test the air temperature. Pulling her foot back in and shivering she cursed as she remembered the only downside to buying this house. Damn heating, she should never have bought a house with storage heaters they were so unpredictable. Emma hated the cold and seemed to feel it easily. It was only the end of October and if the house was this cold now, she couldn't wait until the winter snow came. Brrrr! Maybe she should look at calling in a plumber to plumb in some reliable radiators.

Slowly Emma rolled out from under the duvet, stretching her slender legs until her feet touched the floor she then began patting around until she found her slippers. Then came the hard part, Emma quickly released the rest of the duvet from around her body, getting over to the door to the bedroom and grabbing her oversized towelling dressing gown off the hook. Shivering, she pulled the soft fluffy white material tightly round her and tied the belt round her slim waist.

Time for my morning fix of caffeine Emma thought and headed downstairs to the kitchen.

Once in the kitchen, Emma filled the kettle with enough water for one, flicking the switch on the radio as she walked past it on her way back from the sink and then grabbed her favourite mug off the draining board. It said "Warning - Not a morning person - Come back in the afternoon!" Then, as 'You Win Again', the Bee Gees latest hit single sounded out from the portable cassette radio speakers she headed to the front door to get the milk in for her cereal. Emma was about to open the door when the headlines of the local newspaper caught her eye.

ROSEHILL RAPIST STRIKES AGAIN!

"Jesus," she said to herself, "haven't they caught him yet!"

Emma opened the door and bent down to pick up the milk feeling a blast of chilling air make its way down the front of her dressing gown. Wolf whistles radiated from across the street where the workmen had stopped for a tea break.

Emma consciously pulled together her dressing gown and shouted, "Haven't you got work to do!"

There was a chorus of "Oooooooooooohs" to her statement as she slammed the door and picked up the paper.

After making her breakfast, Emma sat down at the kitchen table, reading the newspaper as she munched her cereal and sipped on her coffee.

"The Rosehill Rapist strikes again. Or does he? Is this just a bad copycat murder? Everything is seemingly the same but why the different area? And why did this girl look different from the others? Has he deviated from his pattern or is there another killer out there willing to take a piece of his homicidal fame?

When asked, Chief Superintendent Bill Wheeler said in a statement, "We've got our best men on this case but with the lack of witnesses, the only leads we have are the similarities in the girl's looks and the way they're killed. This murder follows with some similarities but not all of them. At this stage we have to believe it is the same man. We can't afford not to. Serial killers are known to deviate from their modus operandi from time to time. Police are still questioning people on all the murders, so if anyone did hear or see anything strange on this night or any other night in question, please could they come forward and make a statement. It may not seem like much to you but could be enough to help us locate and catch the culprit."

After reading the paper, Emma went upstairs and took a long soak in the bath. Relishing the feel of the hot soapy water cleansing her skin and turning it lobster pink so much so that she didn't want to leave the steamy warmth of the bathroom. Finally, when the hot water started cool down, she knew she had no choice and ran across the hallway to her bedroom to get dried and dressed as quickly as she could. And as the goose bumps stood to attention on her bare flesh, Emma made another mental note to start saving to get the heating changed.

Emma finally decided what to wear and put on her skin-tight blue jeans with a baggy red sweatshirt. Tucking it into her jeans she checked herself in the mirror. Her figure wasn't too bad considering her favourite pass time of late was snacking on chocolate. Every 'single' ladies dream night in was with a bottle of cabernet sauvignon and a large bar of Galaxy chocolate. As a teenager, Emma had suffered with acne and the boys had given her a wide berth but now the acne had gone, she still wasn't having much luck in the man department. It wasn't that she didn't have any offers Emma was just super picky, after-all she didn't want to end up in a relationship like her mum and dad's. Emma had been told so many times that she could be a model and with her shoulder-length, shiny, dark-brown hair and slender figure and she probably could of if she hadn't been short of four inches of height. If she just had those extra inches then she wouldn't be starting a job in the local bar tonight, that's for sure. Unfortunately, dreaming didn't pay the bills and with a place of her own she needed to earn.

Speaking of bills, she thought, I'd better go and get my groceries so I don't starve next week.

Emma grabbed her denim jacket and trainers on the way out and walked to town, glaring at the workman on the way past who seemed to have heeded to the earlier warning as not a single wolf whistle past their lips. On shopping days she wished that she had a car, sometimes she'd get a taxi home but it proved to be a bit expensive at times so she'd only use one if it was washing powder week. Unfortunately, it was the only way to get home for someone who couldn't afford a car as taking a bus was a nightmare if you had more than two bags of shopping. At least with the new job she should hopefully be able to save up for one. Jackie had a great little white Escort mark 3. It was a sporty looking car and whenever they went out in it, music blaring out the speakers, it turned men's heads. Maybe she'd be able to afford one of those eventually. Emma couldn't believe that she was spending the money before she'd even earned it but wasn't that the way of the eighties economy. It's was all about possessions and 'keeping up with the Jones'.

Emma arrived home at about quarter to one, after procrastinating around a few shops prior to tackling the busy supermarket. She'd just finished putting away her shopping when the phone rang.

"Emma, hi it's Jackie. Where have you been? I've been ringing you for the last couple of hours."

"Hi Jackie, I've just got back from shopping. Town was really busy and the bus was a nightmare as usual. What's up doc?"

"Just ringing to see if you're ready for tonight?" Jackie asked.

"I'm a bit nervous but I'll be okay. I'm lucky to get a job working with my best friend." Emma said smiling inside at that comforting thought.

"Well don't worry," Jackie said, "I made sure that Geoff scheduled me in for tonight and told him I'd show you the ropes. It's going to be great fun, the two of us working together again. Just like when we were at college and working in the local Woollies. I'd offer you a lift but I'm starting earlier than you tonight, so I'll see you later on."

"Yeah, see you later, alligator." Emma said,

"In a while crocodile." Jackie replied with a giggle and with that they both hung up.

Jackie and Emma had been best friends since High School. They'd both taken O levels in Textiles together, getting to like each other on their very first class, they'd been thick as thieves ever since. They'd then both gone to college to study fashion and design. They were going to open their own boutique and become famous fashion designers but as most teenagers do, they left college before even finishing the course both having a change of heart. Now Jackie worked in the local bar and Emma was going to join her. As was the pattern of life, strangely theirs seemed to be moving in the same direction, for the time being anyway.

Emma wore her long hair down most of the time but tonight, for practicality, she decided to wear it up in a Banana Clip. After sorting her hair and make-up out, she got dressed in her 'uniform'. Jackie had designed it especially for Geoff the manager. It consisted of a trendy 'Geoffrey's' shirt which was black with neon green lettering and short black pencil skirt.

Emma left home at five-forty, leaving herself enough time to be there five minutes early. She took the short cut alley that ran through between her road and the road that 'Geoffrey's' was on. Another good reason to be working there, it was only a heartbeat away from home. When Emma arrived, she knocked on the door and waited. She could hear several bolts and latches clanking and then finally a key turned and the door opened.

"Hi Emma," the manager said, "Welcome to Geoffrey's. Ready for some work?" He was a stocky built man in his early forties, very wide and very tall.

"I think so Mr Budd."

"Oh please, call me Geoff," he said grinning like a child as he eyed her up and down, "We're on first name terms here. If you take a seat by the bar, I'll go find Jackie to show you the ropes. Won't be a minute."

"Thanks." Emma said taking a seat on one of the bar stools.

"Jackie!" Geoff yelled as he disappeared out through the door behind the bar. From the slight abdominal protrusion Geoff looked like he enjoyed a good beer and takeaway. He had dark hair, which was slicked back with gel, shiny blue eyes and with red glowing cheeks that reminded Emma of the Santa Claus on the front of Christmas cards. Every time she'd been in for a drink he'd seemed like a very friendly chap, leaning on the bar chatting with her while she'd wait for Jackie to finish, so when Jackie had mentioned that one of the ladies had left and they needed someone to replace her, she'd nearly bit her hand off for an interview. She'd had her fair share of unfriendly workplaces, Emma decided it was time she worked somewhere the boss was more laid back.

Emma took a look round the pub. Neon signs of different descriptions were littered about the walls in no particular order. A large jukebox stood in one of the corners also with neon lights flashing. It was a fairly modern place despite the old fashioned wall paper, which was a maroon and gold pattern to match the heavy maroon velvet curtains and maroon covered stools and benches.

"Hey Emma, see you didn't change your mind about working in the madhouse then."

49

Emma turned round and saw Jackie standing in the doorway over the other side of the room.

Jackie was what most people would call a 'big-boned' girl and Jackie was proud of the fact. She had bleach blonde hair, which was styled, in a short curly bob, similar to Madonna's 'like a virgin' look. Jackie had begun to style her hair with extra curly volume to give the illusion that she was taller than she actually was, which was approximately five foot nothing in socks. Jackie still enjoyed fashion and you could tell by the way she dressed but instead of being a fashion designer, Jackie was now training to be a make-up artist and went to college one evening a week to do so. And this was where the similar pattern of life took different directions for Emma and Jackie, as Emma wasn't sure what career path she wanted to follow.

As best friends, they'd always got on really well and had no secrets from one another. Even if they tried to, one would always seem to know what the other was thinking, which was a real challenge when it came to surprising each other with Christmas and birthday presents.

Jackie was a bit of a comedian at times, they had plenty of laughs together and, Jackie, being the adventurous type would always get Emma into trouble. There was the time they had lit cherry bombs in the toilets at the school disco. Jackie had left one on the windowsill. The window had blown out and the glass had landed on the headmaster's car. Luckily they'd never got caught for that one but there were often phone calls to parents to arrange meetings to discuss their problem children. Even the parents had taken it upon themselves at one point to have a meeting and try and keep them apart but it hadn't worked. Those were the days! No worries and no hurries, was what they used to say. But it seemed as life went on more hurries and more worries would present themselves, despite how much you tried to fight against it.

"Well are you ready to learn?" Jackie asked.

"Yep, ready, willing and, hopefully, able." Emma said with a big grin.

Emma followed Jackie down the cellar to collect some of the bottled beers and fruit juices. When they came back up Emma couldn't help but notice the recognisable smell of Hugo Boss in the bar area. As they walked in she saw Geoff talking with a tall, broad shouldered blonde guy. Emma had seen him when she'd been in for a drink before but had not been introduced, mainly because Geoff always seemed to corner her in with his chat as soon as he saw her enter.

"Ahh here she is!" Geoff said grinning, "Our new girl."

The guy extended his hand to Emma as if to shake it, "David Jessop but you can call me Dave."

Emma extended her arm out to shake hands, Dave took her hand in his but instead of shaking it he turned it over and smoothly planted a quick kiss on the back.

"Emma Parker," Emma giggled, "It's nice to meet you Dave."

"I believe the pleasure is all mine, Miss Parker." He said grinning like a Cheshire cat, blue eyes sparkling.

"Ignore him," Jackie piped up, "He thinks he's the charmer of all women, the master of seduction and believes that no woman can resist him. Shamefully, none of that is true and that's why you're still single, isn't it Dave?"

"Thanks Jackie, I always knew I could count on you to make me feel better!" Dave said sticking his tongue out at her only to have Jackie return the compliment with a couple of fingers added.

"Now, now children," Geoff said, "No time for fighting. We open to the hoards of thirsty punters in a few minutes, so let's get everything stocked and ready to go. I fancy a pint before the doors open, so Jackie, go show Emma how to pull a pint of Fosters."

The end of the shift came quickly for Emma. She was kept quite busy learning lots of new things, meeting the regulars and making a lot of new friends. With time going so fast, Emma wondered if she had really taken in everything she'd been shown.

Every so often, Dave or Geoff would pass a compliment on her work. They seemed to be in competition with one another, no sooner had one passed a compliment then the other was upon her trying to better the last. She guessed they'd calm down as soon as they got used to having her around the place, although she secretly hoped that Dave wouldn't. He was definitely her type when it came to looks whether he would measure up in others ways she guessed she would find out because it had always been her policy not to date work mates in case it went wrong.

Emma was so tired when she got home; she barely had the energy to take her clothes off before falling into bed. She now realized why, whenever she went out shopping with Jackie, it was always in the afternoon. It was so Jackie could catch up on her sleep. Still, she couldn't believe how much she'd enjoyed herself and, although tired, she couldn't wait until her next shift. Maybe this was her next career direction.

Emma had just drifted off to sleep when the phone was rang. She picked it up and held it to her ear. Still on the verge of dreaming she only just managed to say hello into the receiver. Emma listened carefully and started to wake up when she had just the sound emptiness and no answer. "Hello." She said again, sitting up in bed as if that action would improve her hearing. There was still no answer, just the sound of a distant car followed by the click of the receiver being placed down at the other end of the line. 'Must be a wrong number' she thought as put the receiver down and snuggled back under the duvet.

As she was just getting comfortable, the phone rang again. Emma answered it but again nothing was said. As she listened carefully she could hear the sound of someone breathing. Emma shivered as goose bumps rippled down the back of her neck making her hair stand on end. She put the receiver down and reaching down behind the bedside table she unplugged the phone then rolled over pulling the duvet over her head to block out the ringing from the phone downstairs.

Chapter Three

Emma had been working at 'Geoffrey's' bar for three weeks now. She knew all there was to know about working in a bar. Geoff was very pleased with how quickly she'd picked up the job and her dedication to her work.

Emma had made loads of new friends and Geoffrey's bar felt like home from home but, it seemed, she had also made an enemy. She didn't know who it was but someone had been ringing her up at all hours of the night. The phone would ring and she'd say hello once or twice and then whoever was on the other end would hang up. Sometimes she wouldn't even pick it up she would let it click to the answer machine but no one would leave a message. About two minutes later it would ring again making her think it was an important call. It meant that every time the phone rang she'd jump and the lack of sleep had driven her crazy.

The worst thing about it was that if Emma listened carefully enough she could hear someone breathing before the phone was returned to the receiver. That was the only way that she could tell that someone was there. It had made her so nervous at work that she'd started scanning everyone who walked in to see if they looked suspicious. It didn't stop at home either, Emma had found herself jumping when the phone in the bar rang too, just in case it was the same caller, although she'd not once received a silent phone call at work.

Apart from that she was getting hardly any sleep and that hadn't gone unnoticed. Jackie collared her at work one evening and asked her what was wrong. Normally Emma would have been able to keep her cool and dismiss the question but on that night she was shattered from the lack of sleep and broke down, telling Jackie all about the phone calls she'd been receiving.

That was last Tuesday. It was now Monday and Emma had changed her number like Jackie had advised, she hadn't known that you could do it for free if you were receiving nuisance calls. The calls had stopped but that didn't stop her wondering who it was. And as she thought about her nuisance caller, she glanced at the newspaper and began to read.

"No sign of the Rosehill Rapist. Three weeks since his last murder and police are still baffled. It seems like he just vanished into thin air, nobody seems to have seen or heard anything that could have any connection to any of the murders. Police are still appealing for more witnesses to come forward. If you have any information please could you call Ipswich Police Station on..."

Emma looked out of the window. It was still raining and it was her day off but she decided to go for a drink at 'Geoffrey's' anyway. It was normally dead on a Monday night so they might be glad for the business, even if it was an employee.

Anyway, Emma didn't fancy the thought of staying in on her own, even though she had changed her number the phone still made her jump when it rang. At least she'd be able to relax there and she could really do with a good chat with Jackie about what had happened in the cellar with Geoff yesterday. Emma got her coat and shoes on, grabbed her umbrella and headed down the road to 'Geoffrey's'.

As always, Emma took the shortcut down the alley that connected her road to the road that the pub was on. It was lined with brick walls that enclosed the gardens either side. It was fairly well lit with the usual yellowy-orange glare of street lamps. A couple had recently been vandalized as had a lot of things in this area of Ipswich. Unsurprisingly, one of working ones lit up the alleyway graffiti that had appeared a few days ago. Most people were annoyed by it but Emma quite liked it. Just because it wasn't hung in a gallery, didn't mean it wasn't art. Emma especially liked the cartoon-like characters which made her smile, probably some a kind of self-portrait by the anonymous artist. The alley had now become her shortcut to work every day and each day she liked to see if anything new had been added to the walls. Emma couldn't believe her luck when she'd first noticed the alley as it was quite well hidden and someone new to the area would assume it was just a path leading to the back yard of one of the houses. It cut her journey time to 'Geoffrey's' down to five minutes instead of twenty.

When she entered the bar there were a few more than usual in there and not bad for a Monday night. Of course, the usual bunch of regulars were in there, like old Tom with his Jack Russell Terrier cross, funnily enough called Jack, asleep at his feet. He always came in to get away from 'Mrs Tom' and her constant moaning about what the characters in Coronation Street should and shouldn't be doing. Old Tom said he was getting fed up of constantly reminding her that it was a television programme and not real life! He was sat in his usual corner arm chair, with his usual pint of Guinness on the table next to the usual empty bag of cheese and onion crisps that had been bought for him and the now satisfied sleeping dog, pipe in mouth and reading The Sun newspaper. He mumbled a pipe muffled hello out the corner of his mouth as Emma headed past him to the bar. Emma smiled back and said 'Hi.'

Carl was sat with his latest conquest who was giggling away while he paid her compliment after compliment and she clearly couldn't see the reason behind him doing so. If his plan worked, he'd be back in tomorrow night boasting to Geoff and his other mates about his victory.

Jeremy, the estate agent who had sold Emma her house, was in with his friend Michael. They both smiled and waved her over. Emma smiled back, "In a minute guys, I'll just get a drink."

There were a few newcomers to the bar that Emma didn't recognise. A group of men in their twenties dressed in suit trousers and shirts possibly out on an after work birthday drink.

A couple of skinheads were playing pool in the games room off to the right.

"Hello," spoke a well-recognized voice from behind the bar. "I see you've come in just to see me, and I thank you. What can I do for you tonight then gorgeous?" Dave said, a cheeky grin forming on his face.

"The usual Dave, and no, I didn't come in just to see you. As a matter-of-fact, I came in to see Jackie." Emma said.

"Oh Emma you make me feel so sad, I could cry. Why do you do this to me?" Dave said, pretending to look sad and clutching at his heart as if it was aching.

"Oh leave her alone Dave," Jackie said, "Can't you see she's not interested."

Oh Jackie, you can't see how far from the truth you are, Emma thought, if only Dave *was* interested and not just teasing me. Usually Emma would tell Jackie her feelings but Jackie and Dave were good friends and she didn't want to stir anything up because if she and Dave dated and then split up it would ruin all their relationships.

"Hi, how's it going?" Jackie asked, noticing that Emma looked a bit tired but not saying anything.

"Oh, not too bad I s'pose. I was getting a bit bored of being at home alone with nothing on the television, so I thought I'd pop in for a couple of drinks."

"Still getting those phone calls?" Jackie asked, reading Emma's mind.

"No." Emma replied. "But I still jump every time the damn phone rings, even though I changed my number."

Dave handed Emma her Jack Daniels and coke. She still couldn't believe she was working with this incredibly sexy guy and wasn't allowed to touch.

He definitely spent lots of time at the gym developing those beautiful muscles that stretched out the chest and arms of his incredibly tight t-shirt. He had sandy-blonde hair and stunning blue eyes, and when he smiled Emma always felt a warm feeling pass through her, in fact his smile was enough to turn any woman to jelly. She didn't know why this was, maybe it had something to do with the way his cheeks dimpled up, or maybe it was because his eyes shone like blue topaz, as if he was so pleased to see her.

"I'm just going to have a fag break, won't be long." Dave said to Jackie.

"I'm sure I'll cope," Jackie said, looking round the place. "I'm not exactly rushed off my feet."

"Where's Geoff tonight?" Emma asked.

"Oh, he said he'd got a hot date." Jackie replied.

"That's good because I really need to talk to you."

"What's up?" Jackie asked looking all puzzled.

"Geoff made a pass at me yesterday." Emma said.

"What?" Jackie said stunned.

Emma explained how he'd followed her down to the cellar when she'd gone to change a barrel. She'd just tapped in the new barrel and turned round to find him directly behind her. "He went to kiss me and I pulled away. I told him that I thought he'd got the wrong idea and he didn't seem to handle it very well. He didn't speak to me for the rest of the shift. I don't think I could handle it if he's going to be like that every time we work together."

"I'm sure he was just embarrassed. Men never handle rejection very well. I'm sure he'll have calmed down about it by tomorrow's shift. Anyway, he's out on that hot date tonight, he'll have *definitely* forgotten about it by tomorrow, don't you worry."

"I hope so." Emma replied, not convinced.

Time passed quickly in the bar as Emma sat talking with Jeremy and Michael, so before she knew it, it was quarter to eleven and the 'last orders' bell was ringing.

"Do you want a lift home Emma?" Jackie asked. "If you wait I should be done around twelve."

"No thanks Jackie, I really should be going. I didn't plan to stay here this long; time just sort of crept up on me. Thanks anyway, and thanks for the chat. I'll see you tomorrow." She turned and shouted down the bar to where Dave was. "Bye Dave!"

"See you later sexy!" He shouted back. "Shame I've only got my bike 'cause I'd have given you a lift home and you could have invited me in for a nightcap." He winked at her and grinned.

"That's okay Dave the walk will do me good. Got to lose a few pounds you know!"

"Not from where I'm standing!"

It was still raining when Emma left but only slightly, so she didn't bother to put up her umbrella. She turned down the alley.

When she'd left the bar the jukebox was playing 'Don't leave me this way' by The Communards and now she couldn't get it out of her head. Humming to herself, she got about halfway up there when she was suddenly knocked down to the ground. Her umbrella fell out of her hand and skidded across the floor. It happened so fast that she didn't have time to think about regaining her balance, let alone what was going on.

She was about to scream when a hand covered her mouth and a voice said, "Don't even think about screaming, I've got a knife and I won't hesitate to use it. I can still get my pleasure when you're dead but don't make me kill you 'coz you'll miss out on all the fun!" And with that the voice started laughing.

"I haven't got much money. Please don't hurt me. It's in my coat pocket. I'll get it out for you."

"Shut up! I don't want your money. I've been watching you. I've been watching you for a long time. At the bar, down the shops, at your home..." The man stroked her hair. "You're very beautiful but then so were all the others and they didn't obey so they had to die. You are different though, there's something special about you. Be good and we'll get on just fine."

She looked at the man that was on top of her. He had a balaclava on his head. The kind with separate oval holes outlining both eyes, one for the nose and another for the mouth, just like the bank robbers or the IRA wear in movies.

The street lamp at the end of the alley supplied just enough light to make out the colour of his eyes, piercing blue and cold. Every so often when he turned his head they caught the light and glistened just like melting ice. His lips were stretched into a thin grimace, which outlined a set of teeth, yellowed from smoking. The strong smell cigarettes on his breath confirmed this assumption.

Emma could also smell ale and a slight hint of aftershave, which she seemed to recognize but as he moved the smell of his clothes took over. They smelt musty, like when you get mould in a cold, damp room.

All the things she'd read about rape passed through her mind. All the advice for women she'd seen on television chat shows like Oprah Winfrey, stuff she'd heard from friends and read in magazines. Advice like fight back, don't fight back, scream, don't scream, blow a whistle, run, reason with the man.

Lovely advice but all of the contradictions just made her more confused. It was useless! Fight the man? How could she, he was at least ten times bigger than she was. Blow a whistle? What whistle? Who carried one? And as for reasoning with him, he was an animal, he knew what he wanted and he'd made it clear that he was going to get it even if he had to kill her first.

Just then something glimmered in the darkness. Emma turned to look at it. It was the knife. She could just make it out in the darkness. The blade was about eight inches long and in the handle it had a small stone, like an opal, which seemed to be staring straight at her like a blinded eye.

"You're going to enjoy this. This is going to be fun." He said as he began squeezing one of her breasts.

Emma was so scared, yet so repulsed that she wanted to be sick. She turned to look away and saw a white rosebud lying on the floor beside her.

Remembering all she'd read in the newspaper since she'd moved into her new home, she whimpered, "Oh no! No!" Her voice found again as she struggled in vain to escape.

"No, no, no!" He said. "I haven't finished with you. If you do as you're told, I'll let you go but if you carry on I'll have to kill you. You don't want me to kill you, do you?" He said, lifting up her skirt. He used the knife to cut away the thin elastic strips of her tanga briefs. "Ummm!" He said enthusiastically. His eyes glimmered like a child's would when receiving a bag of sweets. "This is the best bit."

"No, please don't do that. Don't hurt me, please don't." Emma pleaded, turning her face away with tears streaming. As she looked away her attacker, who she knew by the tell-tale white rose as the Rosehill Rapist, thrust into her. It hurt so much. Emma squeezed her eyes tightly shut and decided that the best advice to follow was to lie there and pretend it wasn't happening. Maybe drift off to another world. Oh how she longed to be anywhere, anywhere but here.

Just then the noise of someone running and shouting came to her ears. He quickly withdrew and said, "You've been a lucky girl this time but here's a little something to remind you of me." He slashed the knife down the inside of her thigh. "And there'll be more of that if you tell anyone about me. Remember, I'll be watching you!" He turned and ran back down the alley.

Emma pulled her skirt down and managed to summon enough strength to slide herself across to the wall on one side of the alley. Propping herself up against it, she could feel herself shivering uncontrollably as the blood trickled on to the pavement, mixing with the rainwater and disappearing down the alley. And as the voice, which was filled with concern, got closer, her vision suddenly speckled with grey and white flecks. Then Emma's world finally turned black as she slumped and passed out.

Chapter Four

Tony ran across the road to 'Geoffrey's bar'. He looked at his watch. Ten to twelve. Maybe if he was quick he might catch someone.

He reached the door and started to knock just as it opened.

"Hello," He said, "I was wondering if I could use your toilet? I wouldn't normally ask but I've been out on a birthday bash. I was in here earlier with my mates from work. You know how it is though, curry and booze, and I've really got to go. I mean if it was a number one I wouldn't be worried but a...."

"Eeww! Too much information!" Jackie said, a bit shocked to see someone at the door the very minute she opened it and if he wasn't so good looking then she wouldn't even have said the next thing she did. "Come in but be quiet and quick. I'm not really supposed to let you in after hours and I don't want the boss coming in catching you here." It was her job to lock up tonight. Geoff was still out on his date and Dave had left straight after the last customer had left as he had to get up early tomorrow morning to do his other job.

Hurry up in, Jackie thought as she pretended to do some last minute tidying while waiting for him to come out. The sound of an ambulance siren outside distracted her from her thoughts. Jackie pulled back a curtain to take a look. Suddenly the dark silhouette of man darted past the window, making her jump and she watched him as ran off down the street into the darkness. What is taking him so long? Jackie thought and turned back to the toilet door as if it would make him suddenly appear there quicker. If he doesn't come out soon I'll be getting into trouble with Geoff.

Jackie was stood at the window watching the flashing blue lights of the ambulance go by when Tony came out of the toilet. "What's going on? Sounds like some action."

"I don't know?" Jackie said, "I heard the ambulance first, so looked out the window, saw a man go running down the road and then just now the ambulance went by with its lights flashing."

"It's probably just a punch up. There have been a several fights of late, gang related usually. Hopefully it's not one of my bunch getting into trouble. I'd best go check on them. I am the sensible one in the group. Anyway, cheers for letting me use the toilet," he said politely, "I didn't know if I could've waited until I got home, I live over the other side of town and I've got to make sure that these guys get back ok on the way."

There was moment's silence as they studied each other, and then he asked, "Would you like to go out with me tomorrow night? It's the least I can do. I mean you could lose your job for letting me in here after hours. That's if you're not working." He paused, realising he was stumbling over his words in his excitement and rethought his next approach. "You're not working are you?"

Jackie couldn't believe what he had asked her. She'd only met him two minutes ago and here he was asking her out. She wanted to scream yes but she didn't even know what his name was, and even if he was a hunk, she wasn't going to say yes to a complete stranger.

"No, I'm not working," Jackie replied, "And I would like to go out with you tomorrow night but I've been told not to talk to strangers, let alone go out with them." She couldn't believe she just said that. What was she thinking? Possibly, chances like this didn't come around all that often for a girl like her. Most men just liked the supermodel types and to hell with anything else.

"Well you've already broken one rule, you're already talking to a stranger and you let him into the bar. Anyway, for the record, I'm just a boring old self-employed accountant and my name is Tony. There you go, now I'm not the stranger, you are. And now I think I'd better know you're name. You know, just in case you're a mad axe-wielding murderer or something?"

"Mine's Jackie." She said laughing, "And I guess I'll be meeting you back here at seven tomorrow night then!" Interrupted by the slamming of the back door to the pub, Jackie said, "You'd better get out, that's Geoff coming home and by the sound of the door his date didn't go too well! I'll see you out the front in a minute." Jackie locked the front doors to the pub and stopping at the back door, she shouted up to Geoff, "I'm now leaving Geoff." A grunt came from upstairs that confirmed to Jackie that all had not gone well on his date just as she had earlier suspected. She decided to nip out the back door and made her way round to the front of the pub. Tony was still there, his mates forgotten for the time being.

"So I guess we'll meet here at seven then." Jackie said.

Tony nodded in agreement and started to walk down the street towards a group of men on the corner.

As she got into her car she watched him walk down the street. This is unbelievable, she thought, I can't wait to tell Emma, who'd of thought it a tall, dark, handsome stranger asking to use the toilet at this time of night and then asking me out afterwards. Thank you lord! Shit, what am I going to wear?

Inspector Harris stared at the photos that were sprawled across his desk. It was dark outside now and it had been for quite a while but he hadn't noticed. He was wrapped up in his own little world of dead bodies, rapists and murderers. Thank God he wasn't still married otherwise he'd have had Mary on the phone to him by now, nagging at him. He could just imagine it. Why didn't you call me? Your dinner's spoilt now! How am I supposed to know if you're coming home or not! I'm not a mind reader! Besides you could be dead in a ditch, I wouldn't know!

He guessed it couldn't be much of a life being married to a detective. And here he was, still in front of his desk at Twelve-thirty at night trying to fathom out why all the young women in

Ipswich were being killed. In fact the only women he met nowadays were dead ones.

His damn shift ended hours ago, he should be at home in front of the TV with a beer or better still in the comfort of his bed, a gorgeous woman in there with him would be an added bonus! He couldn't remember the last time he'd felt a woman's silky skin against his own.

He picked up the picture of the fifth girl. She was murdered three weeks ago. And now there was nothing except a body and photos of a body to prove it happened. It was as if the murderer was a magician or something. He just managed to vanish into thin air every time - blended in with the paintwork.

She was a pretty girl, the others were pretty too but she was different. She didn't look the same. They had brown straight hair and she was a curly blonde. They were rounded in all the right places and she had a body that you could tell had done hours at the local gym, plus equal time at the local beauty salon. It was no wonder, she was a high-class call girl and she had to take care of herself. What had prevented her from doing so that evening? It had to be a pimp trying to copy the Rosehill Rapist murders. Maybe he'd wanted her off the scene and chose to copy so he could remove himself from the list of possible suspects when the police came sniffing round.

She was a very high-class call girl. Men paid hundreds in cash for her kind. It was so simple, men called her for sex and she went to them, a bit like a call out pizza service, only for very expensive sex instead. Compared with the other girls she seemed the most likely victim for murder.

The only connection they had was the method of murder. He couldn't be a hundred per cent positive whether this was the Rosehill Rapist or just somebody copying him.

He was confused and going round in circles. He didn't know what to think. The body drop was in a different area. She was a different looking girl. If it was a copycat, wouldn't he have copied every single detail that was written in the papers? And if it was the Rosehill Rapist, why did he stray from his usual type of victims and the area he knew? Had he noticed the high presence of police in the area and moved on? Ahhhh this was driving him insane! Was it the Rosehill Rapist or not? If it wasn't then he had a major problem on his hands. It meant he had two murderers on the loose instead of one.

He read the post mortem report, looking at the picture and comparing the words with the visual. She had a deep stab wound to her chest, which had penetrated one of her lungs. Like all of the other corpses she had 'ROSE' carved across her abdomen but she had been found rolled up in a large rug and dumped well away from the usual places. She was one of the least mutilated out of the five corpses. Had he been disturbed by someone before he'd finished or was it that he just couldn't be bothered? It seemed sloppy, that's for sure.

Victim number three was the worst. Her head and hands had been cut about so badly that they had to use her dental records to find out who she was.

When they had eventually found out, it had shocked him so much that he'd wanted to give up on the case and pass it on to another detective. How could this happen to a single mother of two? A single parent, just like his ex-wife Mary and it could just as easily have been Mary. He was so upset after that, he'd got into his car and driven over to Mary's house and poured his heart out to her.

Even though they weren't married anymore, the split had been quite amicable and they had managed to stay friends. Mary had said that he ought to quit his job if it was going to upset him this much but, as Mary always knew, he went back. He always went back. Was it because he felt like it was his duty or was he just a glutton for punishment? Probably both!

He looked at the photos of the girls before their deaths. They were so similar. All you had to do was remove some of the make-up, style the hair the same way, put them in the same clothes, and they could be sisters, all except number five that is.

Their ages varied, though they all looked about the same. Victim number two was thirty-nine but looked like she could be in her early twenties. Yet Victim number four was seventeen. Only seventeen! What a long life she had!

Maybe he was thinking too hard. His head was pounding and all he seemed to be doing was going round in circles. Finally he decided he wasn't getting anywhere, he needed a break. Just five minutes. Just enough time to have a quick caffeine fix and then he'd get back to it. He got up and walked out of his office into the reception area, and over to the coffee machine. The coffee tasted crap but when it came to this time of the day it provided the caffeine boost he needed and that was all that mattered.

"Superintendent Harris Sir!" Called an urgent voice from across the room, "I didn't realize you were still here."

"I'm always here Colin. It's a well-known fact that when you become a Detective Superintendent, you move into the station.

That's why you get an office. It's a shame that they don't provide you with a bed as well. Anyway what's up?"

"It's the rapist, sir. He's done it again. I've been trying to call you at home. It happened about three quarters of an hour ago now."

"Okay so where the corpse this time?"

"There is no corpse Sir, the girl is still alive. Charlie was doing his rounds and interrupted our rapist while he was doing his job. He didn't catch him Sir but the girl is in hospital at the moment. Her leg was cut up pretty bad but as far as I know she's doing okay."

"Right, thanks Colin, I'll get over there right away. Oh and get me a coffee to take out will you, I'll need something to stop me from falling asleep at the wheel."

"Sir!"

Chapter Five

The next thing Emma knew was that she was in hospital. She was confused about why she was in there. The last thing she remembered was saying goodbye to Jackie in the bar.

She looked around the room, familiar with its crisp white walls, smell of sterilized cleanliness and pleasing-to-the-eye, copies of oil-painted landscapes by an unknown artist that would never make it to the big time. In the corner by the door sat a policewoman. She was young looking, must have been new to the force, with her hair pulled back tightly in a bun, she didn't even look old enough to have left school yet.

"W...Why..." Emma stammered as she tried to sit up. "Ahh!"

"Don't move, I'll go and get a nurse." With that the

policewoman hurried out of the door. Emma tried to sit up again, and with the pain that shot through her leg she remembered what had happened. It all came back to her. The man in the balaclava. The knife's gleaming blade. The rape. The white rose. Her head started to swim and she began to cry.

After a few minutes the door opened, and in came the policewoman with a nurse.

"Hello, I see that we are awake now." The nurse said smiling at Emma as she walked towards her. She was a very stocky woman in a dark blue uniform. Probably the matron. She gave her a painkiller and a light sedative, and turned to the policewoman. "You can try to question her now but it won't be long before the sedative begins to work." She turned back to Emma and asked, "Is there anyone I can call to let know that you are in hospital?"

"There's only my friend Jackie." Emma said omitting the fact that she had parents because the last thing she wanted was them here and she gave the nurse Jackie's number.

"Okay, I'll give her a call and you just lay back and answer some questions for this lovely policewoman."

"Please don't tell her why I'm here." Emma said with panic

in her voice.

"It's okay," The nurse said, "I won't say a thing. It's more than my job's worth." She walked out, leaving Emma alone with the policewoman.

"I know this is going to be painful but I need to ask you some questions so we can catch this man before he hurts anyone else." The policewoman's voice was calm and reassuring. "I'd like to know everything, starting from just before it happened?"

"W...Well I left the bar, 'Geoffrey's bar' that is, just after eleven. I took my usual journey home, up the alley between my road and the road that the bar is on. I always go that way. I got about halfway up the alley when someone pushed me down. He must have been following me but I didn't see him. He pushed me down and...and he...he..." Emma looked away from the policewoman.

"It's okay." The policewoman reassured her. "Do you remember what he looks like or what he was wearing?"

As she asked the question Emma remembered the last thing he'd said to her. "There'll be more of that if you tell anyone about me. Remember, I'll be watching you. Remember. Remember."

Emma started shaking her head. "No! No! I don't

remember!" Emma shouted, "Go away and leave me alone!"

"What's going on in here?" The nurse asked as she popped her head around the door to see what all the shouting was about. Looking at the Emma and seeing what a state she was in, she then turned to the policewoman and said, "I think you'd better leave."

The policewoman looked shocked at Emma's outburst and even more shocked that the nurse was kicking her out of Emma's room.

"But this is an important investigation." The policewoman said. "I have orders to stay with the victim."

"I can't have you upsetting my patients like this, no matter how important the investigation is. She needs her rest, I think you'd better leave and come back tomorrow morning. If you have to stay then you can have a chair outside the door but I won't have you upsetting my patients. Do I make myself clear?"

The policewoman nodded and left, followed by the nurse. Emma lay there for quite a while before the sedative began to work, and when she finally went to sleep, a faceless man with a large shiny knife haunted her dreams.

When she awoke the next morning she saw Jackie in the corner of the room, sitting where the policewoman had sat yesterday evening.

So relieved to see Jackie there, she began to cry. Jackie came over, bringing the chair with her; silently she put her arms around Emma. After a while Emma's tears stopped, not because she wasn't upset anymore but because she had no more tears left to cry.

She told Jackie what had happened. "Don't tell anyone Jackie. I don't want anyone to know, he said he'd kill me if I told anyone!"

"It's all right I won't tell no one unless you want me to, I promise but Geoff is going to want to know why you're not at work. I've already phoned and told him you're in hospital. What should I tell him when I pop in tonight?"

"Just tell him I had an accident. Fell down the stairs and sprained my ankle or something. That sounds believable, doesn't it? Tell him I'll be back at work as soon as I can walk properly."

"Shouldn't I just tell him the truth?" Jackie asked.

"No!" Emma replied, "I can't have anyone knowing, not even Geoff. I feel so stupid. It's all my fault. I should never have walked up that alley so late at night, and by myself. I was asking for trouble."

"You stop right there, Emma." Jackie corrected, "One thing you should get straight in your head is that it wasn't your fault. Women have every right to be able to walk the streets at night without having to have a bodyguard with them, so don't you go blaming yourself for this. No man has the right to do what that animal did to you last night!"

Knowing that Jackie was right but now wanting to accept it, Emma went quiet for a moment and then said, "They haven't said how long I am going to be in here yet but will you come by and see me tomorrow?"

"Yeah, I'll pop in around two. Oh, I brought you in a book to help the time pass a bit quicker while you're in here." Jackie said handing her a thick paperback by Emma's favourite author, Stephen King. "I'd better go now. I've got a hot date tonight with this really sexy guy. We're only going into 'Geoffrey's' but it's better than no date at all. See you tomorrow, and don't worry, I won't tell anyone until you're ready."

"Thanks for coming in to see me, it was good to talk. See you tomorrow!"

On leaving, Jackie noticed a policewoman talking with a guy in a beige Mac. They had been there when she arrived. She hurried out of the hospital into the rain and headed for her car. She still had to get ready to see Tony and she didn't want to be late.

Detective Harris had been in this bloody hospital for ages now. He hated hospitals, all he wanted to do was get in and ask a few questions and get out again. All this waiting around was making him edgy. He'd popped by last night but she'd been sedated after having her leg stitched up. Then when he'd popped by this morning she was sleeping and couldn't be disturbed, so he waited. Around lunchtime then he'd watched a girl go into the room with a book and flowers. Harris wondered if she was a relation or friend. She was in there for ages and now she was finally leaving the victims room hopefully he could get on with his investigation again. He strolled over to the nurse outside the room. "Can I go in now?" He asked brusquely.

"Visiting time is over in five minutes, I'll just see whether she's feeling well enough to see you." She turned and entered the victim's room.

After a short while she came out again. "I'm afraid the she needs her rest. You'll have to come back tomorrow."

"Tomorrow!" Harris was losing his patience fast, "Don't you know we've got a murderer on the loose out there and that *she* could be our only hope for catching him!"

"I'm sorry Sir my main concern is that the patient gets better, now if you'll please leave and come back tomorrow as I have asked." And with that she went back to her duties.

Angrily Detective Harris hurried out of the hospital if he was quick enough he might catch up with the girl who was visiting her. The victim was bound to have told her something but as he got out into the car park, he saw her car pulling out onto the street.

"Damn!"

Chapter Six

The door opened and Emma glanced up from the book that Jackie brought her yesterday. With nothing much else to do, she'd managed to get quite a way into it. King had a special talent for drawing you away from reality and making you part of the story. And if anyone needed to be away from reality now it was Emma.

"How are you feeling today?" Jackie asked as she pulled the chair up to the side of the bed.

"Much better." Emma lied and changed the subject quickly. "How did your hot date go last night?"

"All right," Jackie said happily while grinning like a Cheshire cat. "Tony is a great guy, very polite and very much the gentleman. He brought me a lovely bunch of flowers. Beautiful white roses, and...."

Jackie continued to tell Emma of her date, not noticing that it was only one-sided until Emma started to sniff.

"Oh Emma, I'm sorry. Listen to me carrying on when you're hurt and upset." Jackie said apologetically.

"It's not you Jackie it just seems that everything and anything reminds me of what happened. I'm never going to get over this. I'm never going to be able to lead a normal life again. I really wish he had killed me!" Emma said tearfully.

Jackie couldn't believe it, her friend was usually so strong and full of life, and here she was ready to give up on everything. "Emma, don't speak like that. You're going to get through this, and I'm going to help you. You've got to give it time; it's only been a day. Anyway, I was thinking this morning if you like, I'll move in with you for a while. That way if there's anything you want, I'll be there, okay?"

"Oh Jackie, you can't, the last thing you want is to be putting up with me."

"You'd do it for me! It's the least anyone can do for a friend, especially when it's their best friend. You don't need to be on your own at the moment. Besides, you've always been there for me.

Remember when you stayed round my house for three whole weeks after I'd tried to break up with Pete 'the leech' Wragby. You answered the door and the phone, pretending that I didn't live there anymore. Thank God he finally got the message." Jackie said smiling. "I just hope you can put up with my snoring again!"

Emma laughed. It was a little half-hearted but it felt like the first time she'd laughed in her whole life. "The doctors say that I can go home the day after tomorrow. I've got to come back for some counselling and I can't go back to work for a while though, I've got to stay off my feet and let my leg heal."

"Do you want me to come by and pick you up?" Jackie asked.

"That would be good. Are you sure you don't mind?" Emma asked.

"No not at all."

"How's everyone at work?"

"Oh, they're coping. Geoff is missing you. He keeps asking when his star girl is coming back, and Dave keeps asking how you are?"

"I hope you're telling them that I'm all right. You haven't told them about '*it*' have you?"

"No, I'll never tell anyone," Jackie said crossing her heart at the same time and then carried on, "but it's getting hard though, your story is in all the papers, no name of course but anyone who has got a brain could probably put two and two together, and the truth would be staring them right in the face. Dave keeps saying he's going to come and visit you but I've been putting him off. I'll tell him that you'll be coming home soon and he can see you there. Will that be all right?"

"Yeah, that'll be okay, so long as he doesn't find out the truth."

"Anyway Emma, I'd better be going, I've got to work tonight. I'll see you the day after tomorrow."

"Yeah, see you then, and Jackie, thanks for everything. I don't know what I'd do without you."

"That's okay it's what friends are for." Jackie said smiling, and as she turned to walk out the door she bumped into the policewoman that was standing there. Emma recognized her as the one that had been there yesterday, and she wasn't alone. She was with a very strikingly handsome man in a beige Mac.

Jackie recognized them both from yesterday, they were

standing in the corner when she had walked in and were still there when she left.

"Well hello." Jackie said, "I'm leaving now, which is a bit-of-a-shame now I've seen you." She turned to Emma and said with a wink, "You lucky devil. Don't do anything I wouldn't do." And with that she left, leaving the policewoman and the man in the Mac looking stunned and slightly embarrassed.

"Hello." Said the man in the Mac, smiling. "I'm Detective Superintendent Harris but you can call me Steve and this is WPC Simpson, I believe you met briefly yesterday. I'm in charge of investigating your case and I've come to ask you a few questions. We need you to tell us everything that you can remember about the other night."

Emma looked at the Detective. He was a very tall man, at least six foot five. He had hair as black as coal, and with chocolate coloured eyes, it made a lovely contrast to his olive coloured skin. And just like Detective Columbo, he had a long beige Mac on, the only difference was that his was clean.

"I told the policewoman everything I knew the other day." Emma lied and looked towards the window, it was a terrible view of a cloudy dismal day in Ipswich but she didn't care about that.

"I know you're lying." Steve said. He moved in front of the window and looked straight into her eyes. "Miss Parker, you've got to work with us. We're on your side. If you're scared, don't be, we're here to protect you."

"I don't need your protection I'll be just fine on my own. In a few days everything will be back to normal." Emma said, trying to convince herself more than anyone else.

"Listen to me Emma. Until this man is caught and off the streets it won't ever be back to normal. If you want your life back to normal, then you don't want to be looking over your shoulder all the time to see if he's there. Normal isn't being afraid to walk round the next corner or up the next alleyway or afraid to walk out after dark in case he's there ready to kill you because of what you know. You try telling families of the women and girls who have already died to just carry on like nothing had ever happen. They want to see justice done. They want this man off the streets for good. In fact most of them would probably like to see him dead. We all want the streets of this town back to normal just as much as you want your life to be and we don't want any more innocent women killed because of this animal." And turning to the policewoman, he said, "Come on Bev, let's go."

They walked to the door and he turned back to Emma and

said, "Just remember, the longer you think about it, the more lives are in danger. And don't think that just because you haven't said anything that you're not in danger anymore, because you are. You're top of his list!" And with that little speech finished, he turned and left the room.

Steve hated being so harsh on the victims. It made him look like an ogre and feel as guilty as hell. He could see the hurt in Emma's eyes every time he mentioned about the man but he had to get a result. And if getting a result meant shoving the truth down her throat, that's what he had to do.

He felt strange, it wasn't like him to feel *this* guilty about giving the victim 'The Speech' as they liked to call it at the office but as soon as he'd walked in and seen her looking vulnerable as she was talking to her friend he seemed to have this overwhelming need to protect her.

Anyway, it didn't matter how vulnerable he found her, he had to make her face up to the fact that she wasn't the only one who was in danger. Getting that mad man off the streets was first and foremost in his mind, and to do that he couldn't show he cared about anyone.

Chapter Seven

Emma had just finished packing the few things she had at the hospital as Jackie arrived to take her home. She wasn't even sure if she wanted to go home. Despite the hospital smell and the noisy patients in the other wards and rooms beyond hers, Emma felt safe here. If she needed someone all she had to do was press the buzzer. Would she feel this safe at her house? She knew Jackie would be there for a while but Jackie couldn't stay forever.

"Hi," Jackie said, announcing her presence so as not to make Emma jump. "How are you feeling today?"

"I don't know really." Emma said sadly. "Confused, I guess. My head is all over the place with questions and I've hardly slept a wink as they've rattled around in my brain all night. It all boils down to one question really. Why did this have to happen to me?"

"I don't think that I can answer that one for you." Jackie said, wishing she had the solution to this question and any of the others that were keeping Emma awake at night. If only she had a time machine, Jackie thought, she could go back and stop Emma from walking out the pub door on that dreadful night. A time machine was a perfect answer to a lot of bad circumstances but everyone knew that you could never change the past if changing the past was the reason for you acquiring the time machine in the first place. Just ask HG Wells.

"Come on let's get going, you'll feel a lot better when you get home."

"Jackie?" Emma said, her voice sounding pitiful.

"Yeah?"

"Will you do me a really big favour?"

"Of course, what do you want me to do?"

"I know you said you'd stay for a couple of days but could you stay a little longer, just until I feel safe?" Tears started to well up in her friend's eyes as Emma had to admit her weakness by asking Jackie what must have been the hardest question for a strong and independent woman to ask.

Jackie looked at her. She'd never seen her friend scared before and Jackie knew she couldn't be with her twenty-four hours a day. How was Emma going to cope alone in the house while she was at work?

"Of course I will." Jackie replied, going over to Emma and giving her a big hug. "Anything to help you get through this, besides, you are going to need me there until you can walk without those things." Jackie said, pointing to her crutches.

"I see what you mean." Emma said glumly, trying hard not to fall over as she tried to pick up her overnight bag.

Jackie reached over, steadied her and then grabbed the bag. "You'll get used to them 'Hop-along'. We'll go back to mine and I'll pick up some more clothes and stuff, and when we get back to your house I'll call out for pizza." Jackie said. "My treat!"

"That sounds great. Junk food isn't on the menu here." Emma said with a smile.

"There you go I've already managed to get a smile back on your face and with only the promise of a pizza!"

Jackie asked Emma about her visit from the Detective on

their way home.

"I can't tell the police anything, Jackie." Emma explained, "He said if I tell anyone he'd kill me."

"How's he going to find out? And who's to say that it wasn't more than a threat anyway? He couldn't possibly act on that threat because he has got to know who you are to follow it through. As your best friend, I think you should tell the police and I think you should tell them sooner rather than later."

"I can't take that chance, Jackie. I just can't."

The rest of the journey was in silence with Emma just staring out of the window in a daze. Jackie wished she hadn't said anything but she knew it was for Emma's benefit that she had to be hard on her.

When they arrived at Emma's there was a large oblong-shaped white box on the doorstep waiting for them. Jackie carried it inside and handed it to Emma after she'd made herself comfortable on the sofa.

Emma opened the card attached first. All it said was *"Welcome Home!"*

Emma looked at Jackie as she began to open the box. "I bet

some flowers from Dave or Geoff," she said as smile started to appear on her previously saddened face. It was good to know that the people who cared were thinking about her.

The slide the top of the box off and excitedly put it to one side but as Emma gently divided the tissue paper to reveal the contents, her face went pale and she let out a scream. "How did he know?" She said throwing the box to the floor. "How did he know I was coming home today? Has he been watching me while I was in hospital?" She said, breaking down in tears and trembling.

Jackie looked over to where the box had landed and saw the white roses, that had been inside, scattered across the sitting room floor. She quickly cleared them away and sat down beside Emma. She looked straight at her and said, "I don't care what this man said to you, I think you should definitely call the police now."

Just then the phone rang, startling them both. Emma composed herself and reached over to pick up the receiver.

"Hello." She said.

"Hello Emma, did you like the roses I sent you. A sort-of welcoming home present you could say, or not as the case may be."

"How did you get my number?" Emma said but then like a bolt from the blue she suddenly realizing that he'd called her by name and cried, "How do you know my name?"

"I know your real name too." The voice said. "Now all the niceness is over and done with, what have you done with my baby boy? A boy needs his dad you know. You can't just take him away from his father."

"Leave me alone!" Emma shouted into the receiver.

Jackie grabbed the phone out of Emma's hand. "Who is this?" She shouted but it was too late. As if by some psychic reaction, he'd already put the phone down.

They sat there looking at each other for a few minutes, eyes wide, mouths open.

"Do you think he's watching us now? He is, isn't he?" Emma whispered as if he could hear her.

The silence was broken by the phone ringing again making both girls jump. Jackie went to pick it up but Emma grabbed the receiver first.

"Hello again, I forgot to ask who your lovely friend is. Does she know about me?"

Emma looked at Jackie, wide eyed like a rabbit stuck in the headlights of an on-coming car. He knows your here, Emma mouthed. Jackie froze not daring to move or say anything as Emma cut off the caller by replacing the handset.

"You've got to tell the police Emma." Jackie said, running over and pulling the curtains shut, "You've just got to."

"I can't. He said he'd kill me if I told anyone and if he's watching us, he'll know if I tell the police, then he'll kill us both."

The phone rang again. They looked at each other and Jackie said, "I'll get it this time."

Jackie picked up the receiver. "Hello, who is it?" She asked nervously.

"Hi Emma, it's Dave. How are you?"

"Sorry Dave." She said loudly, looking at Emma and breathing a big sigh of relief. Emma slumped down into the chair relieved it was Dave and not the last caller ringing again. "I'm afraid it's Jackie you're talking to. What can I do for you?"

"Hi Jackie," Dave said, "What are you doing answering Emma's phone?"

"Emma asked me to stay with her until she feels..er..better." She said, hoping not to sound too false.

"I was just calling to see how Emma is? What do you mean

feeling better? You said she'd sprained her ankle." Dave asked with confusion in voice.

"She's all right, just a...umm...tummy bug from the hospital." Jackie answered.

"Can I speak with her please?" Dave asked.

"You'd like to speak with Emma?" Jackie repeated loud and slowly while looking over to where Emma sat shaking her head frantically.

"Yes please." Dave said, getting a bit suspicious.

"I'm afraid she's just this minute fallen asleep." Jackie lied. "Shall I get her to call you back?"

"No, that's okay." Dave replied. "Just tell her I'll pop in and see her before work tomorrow afternoon. Geoff's coming, got to go. Bye!"

"But...Dave!" Jackie started but it was too late. He'd already hung up.

"Do you want the good news first, or the bad news?" Jackie asked.

"The good news first please?" Emma said, looking worried.

"The good news is that was Dave and not our 'friendly' caller from earlier."

"I deduced that one Sherlock, what's the bad news?" Emma asked.

"Well," Jackie said looking at down the floor, "I did my best but Dave is coming round tomorrow afternoon."

"What! Oh, that's just great!" Emma said looking at her bandaged leg. "What am I going to do now?"

"It's OK Emma, we'll sort it." Jackie replied as she pondered over what to do. "Shall we order that pizza now?"

The next day came all too quickly for Emma. And the afternoon came even quicker. The doorbell rang at about two-thirty. Emma had already got Jackie to cover her up with a blanket so that Dave wouldn't see the bandage on her leg and the crutches were placed behind the sofa. Once all the incriminating evidence was hidden Jackie answered the door.

"You still here, Jackie." Dave said sarcastically as he came in. "Can't Emma get rid of you!"

"Hello to you too Dave!" Jackie said. "You'd better come in.

Would his majesty like a cup of tea or something?"

"A something would be nice but only if Emma's up to it." He said jokingly.

"A cup of tea it is then." Jackie said. "She's through there." Heading off to the kitchen to put the kettle on.

As soon as Dave entered the living room he knew something was wrong. Despite the smile on Emma's face, the radiance that normally surrounded her had disappeared and she seemed different somehow. It was like looking at a diamond through a smoky lens.

"Hello!" He said merrily. "How's my favourite lady today then? I hear you've been playing stunt-woman down your stairs."

"I'm fine Dave. It was just a tumble really." Emma lied but felt sure that she hadn't convinced him. "How are you?" She asked, attempting to take his focus off her well-being. It worked for a couple of minutes.

"Not bad. I brought you a box of chocolates. Hope you like them?"

"Well chocolates are my favourite snack, how could you go wrong?" Emma said smiling as she eyed up the well wrapped box.

"At least you've made her smile." Jackie said as she came through from the kitchen bringing the mugs of tea and biscuits in on a tray. "She's been like a bear with a sore bum since I brought her home."

They sat and talked most of the afternoon. Jackie interrupting with something completely bizarre or mindless every time Dave came close to asking Emma about her 'trip down the stairs' or her 'hospital tummy bug'. Along with the chocolates, Dave brought some "Get Well" cards from Geoff and some of the regulars.

Emma tried her hardest to be her bubbly self as much as possible but it was hard to keep up the pretence. Whenever she looked at Dave he always seemed to be asking "What's wrong?" and Emma just kept looking away hoping that he wouldn't mention anything.

In a way she was glad Jackie was there, despite the both of them picking on each other all the time, at least he wouldn't ask her what was wrong while Jackie was there and if he ever got close to broaching the subject, Jackie carried on conveniently steering him in off course with another insult.

When it was time for him to leave, he got up and gave her

kiss on the cheek and whispered in her ear, "I'll come back and see you soon gorgeous."

Jackie showed him next door. "When are you working next?" He asked Jackie.

"Tomorrow night." Jackie replied.

"I'll see you tomorrow night then." And with that he left to start his shift at Geoffrey's.

After Dave had left, Jackie and Emma went into the kitchen and had something to eat. Then they sat and watched a couple of videos that Jackie had rented. Emma enjoyed the films but was somewhat distracted by her thoughts. She couldn't help but contemplate how she was going to continue on with everyday life now that she had been raped. Could she ever move on, forgetting what had happened to her or would she be reminded every day by something different? Unlike a movie, Emma couldn't stop her life if it got too scary. She couldn't put everything on pause or rewind back to the days when things were always happier and men in masks didn't exist.

"Want something to drink?" Jackie said, noticing Emma vacancy and breaking her from her thoughts.

"Yeah, a whisky would be nice but I'll settle for a juice

because of my pain killers."

Jackie had just left the room to get a jug of juice from the fridge, when the phone rang. Emma picked it up. "Hello," said a harsh voice. "I don't like your boyfriend and I don't like the new name you've chosen for yourself either. You're supposed to belong to me Rose. I hope you didn't tell him anything, I'd have to kill you if you did! Just remember, I'm watching you!" And the receiver went down.

Emma had wanted to say something but all she could manage was to open her mouth and when Jackie came back into the room that's how she'd found Emma, sitting there, mouth open and staring out of the window with the phone against her ear.

"Emma, are you all right?" Jackie asked, and when Emma didn't answer, Jackie said, "It was him wasn't it?"

Emma just closed her mouth and nodding vacantly she said, "Maybe I should change my number again."

"Sod changing your number, I'm calling the police." Jackie said reaching for the phone.

Emma pulled it away from her, "No, you can't. He's out there watching us and he'll find out if you do."

"Detective Harris will help you, Emma. He'll make sure you have protection. No one will hurt you."

"I said no! He'll kill us both if he finds out." Emma said putting her head in her hands and sobbing.

Reluctantly, Jackie helped Emma upstairs to bed when what she really wanted to do was walk out and leave her to it but being her best friend she couldn't bring herself to do so. In her room across the hall, Jackie could hear Emma's muffled crying. She wished that there was something she could do but it was best to pretend in the morning that she'd slept all right, and hadn't heard anything if Emma asked. Emma needed to get over this but there was only so much that a friend could do, and letting her have a bit of time to herself would also help. Jackie knew that Emma would come to her if she needed her and when Emma was ready to talk Jackie would be there for her.

Chapter Eight

It had been a couple of months since Emma had hobbled out of the hospital entrance believing that everything would work out fine, that she would able to just put everything behind her and get on with her life as if *it* had never happened. As it stood, life hadn't gone back to normal, she definitely hadn't forgotten what had happened to her and things had gone from bad to worse.

In two months Emma had managed to become jobless, lost her self-confidence and nearly become best-friendless into the bargain. In all this wasn't the *normal* she was hoping to have returned to.

Over the first few weeks Emma found herself making more and more excuses so she didn't have leave the house, then she began putting off things like food shopping and when finally she ran out of something she'd send Jackie out on errands to get bits for her. Emma finally realised that she was actually frightened to leave the house when it came time to go back to work and that was when she had handed in her resignation. Making a very weak excuse on the phone and sending a letter in with Jackie was her way of handing it in. Geoff, who was still unaware of what had happened, had been none too happy about it, ringing up several times before giving up with the idea of telephone contact and trying the only other alternative, a visit. He'd popped round a couple of times to try to get her to come back to work but Emma had either not answered the door or got Jackie to tell him that she was unavailable. This had the knock on effect of Geoff giving Jackie a hard time at work. Jackie had stood up for herself though, telling Geoff that if he didn't stop pestering her about Emma then he would find himself down two bar staff instead of just one. He'd even sent Dave around to try and find out what was going on but Jackie was sworn to secrecy and Emma certainly wasn't going to tell anyone else. Emma just couldn't risk more people being involved.

Anyway with the stress from Geoff and then having to help out Emma with anything she needed outside of the home, Jackie found herself popping to and from her own flat spending most of her nights at Emma's house, except when she wanted some quiet time with Tony of course. Not only was this challenging Jackie and Emma's friendship but was also challenging her and Tony's relationship. Jackie would have loved to have brought Tony back to Emma's flat but she could guarantee what state of mind her friend would be in. One minute Emma was singing as if nothing bothered her, the next, usually following a phone call, she would snap at everything or just hide herself away in her room crying. Jackie was trying to be understanding towards her friend but deep down she thought that Emma needed some help and not just from the police either.

Reaching the two month marker, Jackie had started to lose patience with Emma. Just about every time the phone rang when Jackie was there she'd find herself in an argument about Emma not contacting the police. Then when Emma handed in her notice at the bar Jackie had told her that this couldn't go on and they'd argued about how Emma was going to pay her bills. It was starting to feel like they were married, not best friends. Even after two months Emma was still as stubborn about involving the police as she had been the day she had arrived home from hospital. The phone calls were less frequent now, like he was just checking in but they always knew he was watching because he would mention something going on at the time. He even knew that Emma had jacked in her job at the bar, which made Jackie think that he might be a customer. This put Jackie on edge at work as well as at Emma's and while working she found herself looking at the male drinkers wondering if that person was him or not. If only Emma would just call the police then they may be able to catch him and just put an end to it.

Tonight was no different to any of the others. Just as Jackie was about to walk out the door to go to work that evening, Emma insisted, as she always did, that Jackie took her car. It's funny how the smallest things can be the trigger that sets off the frustration that's been building up inside like the barrels of gunpowder built up under the House of Lords leading up to the 5th of November 1605. This time however. No one was caught before the big bang happened.

"I have no option but to take my car!" Jackie shouted at Emma, who recoiled back into the sofa away from her friend's outburst. "You have given me no other option. I am just as much a prisoner in this situation as you are and I haven't got any idea what this guy looks like, unlike you! I haven't even met this guy so

I can't help the police with their enquiries, unlike you! You could change all this just by making one phone call but selfishly you sit there doing nothing. Pretending that everything is going to be all right while living life behind your rose-tinted glasses!" Jackie walked out the room, grabbing her keys in the hallway. Breathing deeply she stopped by the phone table, picking up the phone book and flicking through it for the Ipswich Police Station phone number then writing it on a scrap of paper she placed it by the phone. Jackie then popped her head back round the living room door and looking sternly at Emma she said, "I don't know what you did with the card from the Detective so I've put the number for Ipswich Police Station by the phone if you don't call them tonight then I will be calling them on your behalf tomorrow. Oh and I will be spending tonight with Tony at my flat." And with that Jackie left for work slamming the front door behind her.

Emma sat there, unmoved from the position she took during the confrontation with Jackie, just staring into space. Her vision blurred the world around her while the quietness of the house became overwhelming and Emma felt imprisoned in this invasive silence. Already, it felt like Jackie had been gone for hours when in reality she'd only been gone about ten minutes. Emma was just about to put on the TV if only to drown out the silence and give herself something else to focus on, when phone rang making her jump.

Nervously she picked up the receiver but before Emma could say hello the all too familiar voice said, "Hello Rose. Oh I'm sorry it's Emma now, isn't it. Would you rather I called you by your old name or your new name? How are you tonight?" He paused to see if she'd say something or put down the phone but Emma had frozen to the spot. "All alone I see. Your boyfriend hasn't come round to see you again today did you tell him not to?" His pauses added a sinister edge to every question he asked making Emma frightened to answer just one of them. "You're a bit quiet is it because I scare you?"

Not wanting to answer that question but knowing she had to say something soon, Emma nervously steered him away from it by asking one of her own, "Why are you doing this to me?"

He could hear from her tone that she was frightened and this made him feel stronger, more satisfied with the situation, more in control. "You know why. You're mine and I want you to come home to me. We both know who you really are and I know that you've just had a small blip and that you really still want to be with me. Be a good girl and go collect our baby from wherever you have sent him and then come back to live with me so we can forget this

113

ever happened. You see if you don't do as I say then you'll leave me no option other than to kill you and that wouldn't be nice for you, would it." This was more of a statement than a question. "Just remember, you belong to me and I'm watching you." And without waiting for a reply he put down the phone.

Emma stood there for a long time just holding the receiver, past events going over and over like a video being replayed in her mind. The rape playing over in her mind like she was out of her body watching it happen. That was followed by what Detective Harris had said at the hospital. Then there was Jackie telling her that she was selfish and she had to tell the police. Between everybody else's input was that of the man who had raped her telling her that he was watching and that he would kill her if she told the police. Emma felt like the figure in Edvard Munch's Scream. Turmoil was tearing through her brain and confusion was reigning. Emma was a prisoner to her own indecisiveness, with each path leading to an uncertain future, which path should she take? She had to choose before her brain exploded under the pressure.

The police had said that they would protect her. He was obviously watching her and he wasn't going to go away. It was evident that he wasn't going to just stop calling her one day and never call again. He thought Emma was someone else. Someone called Rose and he believed this Rose person belonged to him. He wasn't going to stop anytime soon, he was going to keep this up for the rest of his life, or hers. Maybe that was the answer, the only way to stop this nightmare would be to end her own life then Jackie could get back to hers. If only he'd killed her that night then she wouldn't have to go through all of this.

Wallowing in self pity she went into the kitchen and poured herself a hefty shot of Jack Daniels. Taking an equally hefty swig she headed back into the living room. This just wouldn't do. How had she become like this? Before this had happened she would have be thinking just like Jackie. Jackie was right; it was selfish not to tell the police Emma had to think of the others he'd already killed and the others that he may hurt.

Detective Harris was right; she could never lead a normal life while he was still out there on the streets. Emma couldn't let him get away with this. How many others would he rape and kill if she didn't tell anyone? If she did tell though, and he found out, he'd kill her for certain. Emma was pretty sure that he'd find out, he knew always knew everything that was going on and she didn't want to die but she had to take a chance that he wouldn't find out.

Eventually Emma picked up the phone and dialled the

number for Ipswich Police Station and after putting the receiver down twice as she argued with herself some more, she finally managed to stay strong and hold on for an answer. "Hello, I'd like to speak to Detective Superintendent Harris please."

"Who's calling please?" asked a polite if not slightly mechanical voice at the other end of the line.

"Emma Parker."

"If you'll hold for just a minute, I'll put you through."

It was only a few seconds before he answered but to Emma it felt like an age, that was only made to feel more uncomfortable by the classical music being played just to let you know that you were on hold and hadn't been hung up on. When finally a voice came it was so sudden that Emma nearly dropped the receiver as she jumped out of her skin.

"Hello Emma, how can I help?" Harris asked already knowing what she was going to say.

"Please help me. He's watching me." Emma said, the strain coming through in her voice. "He's phoning me and saying things that don't make any sense. I thought I could cope but I can't and I'm sorry I didn't tell you everything at the start but I was scared. I still am scared. Please help me Detective."

"It okay Emma, I'll come over right away." Harris said.

"No, you mustn't come over. He's outside the house somewhere. He's been watching everything and he said kill me if sees me telling anyone."

"Okay, I'll wear something inconspicuous and bring you some flowers, like a well-wisher. Please don't worry, I will help you and he won't even know that I am. I'll see you in about half an hour." And with that he put the phone down.

Emma paced the floor by the front door in her mind while waiting for him to turn up. In reality she sat on what she called 'the coat chair'. She still hadn't got round to putting up the coat hooks that she'd bought straight after she'd moved in and as a temporary measure the chair had been placed there and there it stayed, like a lonely dog waiting by the door for its owner to come home. Emma drummed her fingers on the wooden arm just so the silence wouldn't drive her mad while she waited.

After a while Emma decided that the drumming was having the opposite effect to what was desired and decided to call Jackie to let her know what had happened. Not only did this make her feel better but it took her mind off the time while she was waiting for Detective Harris to come. Jackie asked her if she wanted her to come home but Emma assured her that she would be all right. It would just look like something was up if she did.

"I'm sorry I didn't listen to you Jackie." Emma apologised.

"I'm glad you've finally come to your senses." Jackie said, relieved.

Just then the doorbell rang.

"Got to go now Jackie, he's here. I'll see you tomorrow. Have a good night with Tony." Emma put down the receiver and went to answer the door.

Chapter Nine

"They're beautiful. Would mind getting down a vase for them? They are up there," Emma said as she pointed out the cupboard where the vase was kept, "I'm still not allowed to go climbing and stuff because my leg's not quite healed. Usually I would use the steps to get one down."

Detective Harris locating the correct cupboard asked, "Which one would you like?"

"I reckon I'll need the round one. They really are beautiful."

Finding the correct vase he then proceeded to un-wrap the cellophane from around the flowers and, with little thought to arrangement he placed them in the vase and added water from the tap.

"I'm not really good at this sort of stuff. I don't really have cause to buy many flowers." He said trying to break the ice.

"That's fine, they look lovely." Emma said grateful that they were lilies and not white roses. "You should give up being a detective and open a flower shop." Emma said trying to make light of what she knew was going to be difficult discussion.

They headed into the living room. Detective Harris sat down on the sofa whilst Emma hobbled to the chair by the window, stopping only long enough to look around the immediate area outside before closing the curtains and sitting down.

"Detective Harris, I really don't know where to start."

"Well, you can start by calling me Steve." He said with a smile that hoped would get rid the restlessness Emma was clearly feeling.

Emma smiled and took in a deep breath, "Ok, Steve it is. Firstly, I have to apologise. I've been stupid I should have spoken to you from the start. Instead I've been putting up with phone calls from him saying that he's watching me and watching the news to make sure that no one else has been hurt by him. I've been living in my kitchen mostly. If I'm in here I close the curtains. Sometimes, I look out the window to see if he's out there. I even find myself wishing that I could see him, just so I'd know that he is there. Sometimes I see a shadow and convince myself that it is him just so I don't go mad wondering if it is. Does that sound crazy to you?" Emma was surprised at how calm she felt while she was telling him about the phone calls.

"Well, why don't we start with a description of what he looked like, what he was wearing, things like that may help you to remember more? We've already got the details of what happened."

"Okay. Well he wore a balaclava that covered most of his face. His mouth was showing, and I could just about see his lips. They looked like normal lips to me not much I can describe to you about those." Emma took another breath and remembered a bit more. "His teeth, he had yellow teeth and his breath smelt of stale alcohol and cigarettes. Kind of like the slop pot that we have...had at the bar." Emma looked to the ceiling and closed her eyes. "The balaclava had a hole that outlined both his eyes at once. Like the kind you see them wearing on an S.A.S film. It was his eyes that I remember most. His eyes were light blue, like glacier ice and the colour was so cold it was like...oh...I've just remembered, he had a strange knife. It was really shiny, well looked after and was intricately carved, maybe antique with a large stone, similar to an opal, set in the middle of the handle. That's all I can remember, apart from the rose, that is. When I saw the white rose, I remembered what I'd read in the paper. I thought I was going to die." It was then Emma resolve finally broke and she started to cry. "And now I know he's watching me, I'm sure that one day he's going to kill me. Not just yet though, he seems to be enjoying it."

"By 'it' you mean the phone calls?" Steve interrupted. "Can you tell me more about the phone calls?" Steve asked, calmly, fighting the urge to go over and take her in his arms. Maybe, in hindsight, he should have sent one of the other detectives, one of the women. They would have been able to deal with this a lot easier than he could. He always went weak around good looking women, especially the vulnerable ones.

Emma looked round the room blinking back the tears. Then taking another deep breath and composing herself, Emma said, "Well, I've been having the odd phone call off him every now and then since I came home from hospital. It started with a box filled with white roses being left on the doorstep. We found them when we got home from the hospital. Then he phoned me up after I'd opened the box just to make sure I'd got them and to let me know that he hadn't forgotten me."

"We?" Steve questioned.

Interrupting seemed to a special talent for the Detective, Emma thought. "By 'we' I mean Jackie and I. She brought me home from the hospital and carried the box into the living room."

"OK. I'm right by saying that you haven't kept the box as it was a couple of months ago now?" Steve asked, knowing it was pointless asking but he had to do so, just in case.

"Sorry, I got Jackie to throw them out straight away."

"I should have a chat with Jackie to see if she noticed anything strange when you got back. Go on tell me more about the calls."

"When he calls he asks me all the time if he scares me and tells me that he's watching me."

"How can you be sure that he's watching you? He may be saying it just to scare you. He seems to like the thought of you being scared."

"I know he's out there watching me because my friend Dave came round the other day and he phoned me just after Dave had gone to say that he didn't like my boyfriend. He always mentions something that's happened prior to when he phones."

Steve nodded, it was no wonder Emma tried to stop him

coming over.

"What puzzles me the most is that he keeps saying he knows my *real* name and sometimes he asks what I have done with his baby?"

"That maybe his motive for doing what he is doing."

"Can you help me, please? I feel like I'm losing my mind. Every time the phone rings I leap like Sylvester the Cat in the Looney Tunes cartoons. I don't want to answer it in case it is him but then I don't want to leave it in case it's a friend. I haven't been out of the house since coming back from the hospital. I feel like a prisoner trapped in my own home."

"It's okay Emma we will get some surveillance posted outside your house watching you day and night from now on. It won't take long to set it up. We'll have one man follow you whenever you want to go out. It'll be a different man each time, so if he is watching you, then you can relax because he'll just think it's someone who happens to be passing at the time."

It was Emma's turn to interrupt this time, "How will I know it's your guys following me and not him?"

"These undercover guys are very good at their job. You will just need to call us to say you're leaving the house and we'll sort out a signal before you leave. Also, if it's ok with you, I would like to try a new piece of equipment out. It may help us to trace the calls he makes and we could catch him that way."

"I'm willing to try anything. I just want him to stop." Emma said.

"I shall get someone to phone you every day at nine in the morning, noon and nine in the evening. You'll have to use a code to let us know that you are all right."

"Why shouldn't I be all right? You just said that I'd be safe!" Emma said, alarmed.

"It's just a precaution. Let's see now, what would make a good code?" He looked around the room as if for inspiration. "I know," He said, looking towards the two smiling cat ornaments that were sat on each end of the ornate mantelpiece. "The cat is still smiling."

"The cat is still smiling!" She repeated, "I'm going to feel really silly saying that."

"That's why it's necessary, because if, and I mean IF, you're in trouble, you'll be too scared to remember to say it. If he's got you hostage in here when I phone you, he'll tell you to pick up the phone and say you're all right but he won't know the code, and that's how we'll know that you're in trouble."

Suddenly, they heard a rattling at the front door. Steve got up and pulled a small revolver from a holster under his trouser leg, and ran round to the front door. He pointed his gun straight at the door and said, "Come in real slow!"

"Detective Harris I presume?" Jackie said as she peered round the door. "Really inconspicuous!"

"I'm sorry," He said, "I thought you might be the rapist."

"I'm sorry to burst you bubble Mr Detective but I'm sure that the rapist in question has a dick, and I don't think that he has a key to get in." She said sarcastically, waving the door key in front of his nose.

Emma hobbled into the hallway. "I'm sorry Steve, I told you that my friend Jackie has been helping me out since I left hospital but I forgot to tell you that I have given her a key." Emma looked at Jackie, "I thought you were out with Tony after work?"

"I know but he couldn't make it and after your call I thought I would come back and check up on you. Couldn't let you have the Detective all to yourself now could I?" Jackie turned to Harris, "I'm Jackie, pleased to meet you, even if it is in such a strange way."

"Yes, nice to meet you too." Steve said smiling, "Anyway I think I'd better be going now."

"Something I said?" Jackie asked.

"No, not at all." He turned to Emma. "Remember the code! I'll see you soon."

"That sounds mysterious?" Jackie said quizzically as she shut the front door.

"Oh, it's nothing for you to worry about." Emma laughed.

"He's a nice guy, Emma. That's the sort of man you want to go for. He'll protect you, He's got a sexy body, and even better still, he has a good job with a nice fat pay cheque at the end of every month. Why I think I could go for him myself if I wasn't seeing Tony that is."

"Oh Jackie, is men, sex and money all you ever think about?"

"Yes but not necessarily in that order!" She said grinning cheekily.

Laughing, they both went into the kitchen to get a bit of cheese of toast for supper and, while eating, Emma explained what Steve was going to do.

He stood directly across the street in the alley that led to the back gardens of the terraced houses. No one could see him there. It was pitch black now. He stood there just watching. He had watching from his car just down the road when he had seen the short dumpy one leave the house and get in her little Escort, possibly going to work. He knew they had worked together and he knew the short dumpy one was called Jackie.

It was then that he had gone to the nearest phone box to make his phone call. It was good to hear her voice. To hear how scared he made her. He always tried to call her when she was on her own. She always sounded more scared then.

After the call he'd come back and decided to scoot down the alleyway where he stood now as it had a pretty good view into her living room window. Shortly after taking up the position he saw a man carrying some flowers walk up the path to her door and she let him in. He felt a jealous pang from the pit of his stomach as he watched her let him in. She had looked pleased to see this man. Was he another boyfriend?

Shortly after he'd entered she'd drawn the curtains. This made him mad. After a couple of hours the short dumpy one known as Jackie returned and as she entered the house, noticeably slowly to ensure everything was finished. It was obvious what he was there for because after her return, he'd left. What a complete and utter whore she had become.

He stood there watching, fighting the urge to call her again, waiting in the alley until they both went to bed and the lights went out, and then he finally went home.

Chapter Ten

Steve swirled the last dribble of coffee around in his cup. This was not like him at all. All he'd done since he arriving at work this morning was think about Emma. Even his coffee reminded him of her. He drank his coffee milk free and the colour of it reminded him of her gorgeous dark-brown hair. He could imagine it sprawled out over the pillows on his bed; all shiny and smooth like strands of silk. He imagined that he had red silk sheets and pillowcases. The contrast between her hair and the pillows would be so beautiful. Just like her. He imagined her speaking his name in a seductive tone and asking him to make love to her. Laying there on his bed, naked, ready for him to take her in his arms and make love to her. Now all he was ready for at this moment in time was to take a cold shower. He wondered what she was doing now.

Emma awoke to a knock at the door. She looked at the clock. It was two in the afternoon. She must have dosed off. It was understandable though, she hadn't had a lot of sleep lately. The knock came again. It couldn't be Jackie because she'd only left for work a couple of hours ago, and she wasn't due home for ages. Anyway, she had a key.

Emma went to the front door and looked through the peephole that Steve had her install. It was Dave. What was he doing here? It had been a couple of days since she'd seen him but he hadn't called to let her know he was coming. He was going to notice something was up. Emma wasn't ready for him to visit her but she couldn't ignore the fact that he was there. He knew she was in. She'd be all right if she played cool. If he made any remarks about her she'd ignore them.

He knocked again, this time a bit louder. She opened the door.

"Hi Dave, nice to see you. You must be psychic, I was just beginning to get bored sitting here on my own."

Dave noticed her voice was high pitched and she had false

grin on her face and that wasn't all he noticed, for example, all the fresh locks and the peephole that had been installed since his last visit. "What's all this for?" He asked, and trying to hide his concern, he joked, "Been playing Fort Knox with Jackie!"

"What?" Emma asked, knowing full well what he was talking about but pretending not to all the same.

Now he definitely knew there was something wrong, she'd missed his joke completely. "All these locks and a peep-hole? Expecting trouble?"

"Oh those," Emma said, trying to think of something to say without giving any indication of the real reason. "Just a precaution. The crime rate is on the rise and there have been a couple of thefts down the road. Better to be safe than sorry."

"Get the kettle on then!" He smiled, he wasn't going to push her into telling him the real reason, and he had more important things to talk about than that.

They both went into the kitchen and she put the kettle on.

"What are you limping for?" Dave asked, suddenly.

"Full of questions today, aren't you?" She said, stalling time to think of an answer. "I sprained my ankle on the stairs yesterday. So silly of me really, Jackie and I were mucking around, and I slipped. Easily done." Emma lied as best as she could but it sounded so false. Too false!

"You have been in the wars a lot lately, haven't you! Maybe you should see to those stairs." Dave said pretending to believe her, so she wouldn't get upset.

"Would you like some biscuits?" Emma asked, changing the subject.

"Yes please." Dave said. "What's a cup of tea without some biscuits to dunk in it?"

Emma hobbled over to the cupboard where she kept the biscuits and took them out. She turned around to find Dave standing directly behind her. She looked up at him. She could feel his blue eyes staring straight into hers as if probing for something. Slowly his head came down and his lips brushed delicately against her lips, as if finding their way, and then getting harder, the kiss became more ardent. The biscuits, now forgotten, fell out of her hand and rolled across the floor. It was one of those kisses that had so much passion it made you long for more, never wanting it to end. Although, it was nothing like the ferocity of the rape, still, it popped into Emma's mind like storm disturbing the peace and tranquillity of a picnic. She pulled away from Dave and walked over to the kettle, which was now beginning to boil.

Dave bent down and picked the packet of biscuits up. "I'm sorry, I shouldn't have done that." He said, going back to his seat and sitting down. Opening the biscuits he said, "I must have been getting the wrong signals because clearly you don't feel the same way as I do. I should have told you first. Now I've ruined everything."

"Told me what?" Emma asked, staring at the two cups of tea and knowing exactly what he was going to say and wishing that he wouldn't.

"Emma, I have a confession to make. I don't know how to put it, or how you're going to take it, especially now, after what's just happened. I think I just got my answer but here goes anyway."

"Don't say it Dave."

"No, I have to. I'll get straight to the point. Emma, I think, no, I know, I'm falling in love with you. From the minute that you walked into work..."

"You can't!" Emma blurted out, dropping the cups of tea over the floor. "You can't love me!" And she hobbled out of the kitchen as quickly as her leg would allow, going upstairs to the safety of her room and slamming the door behind her.

Dave sat there astounded for a moment. Where the hell had that come from? He expected maybe, 'Get a life!' or 'You're a nice guy but...' He certainly wasn't ready for that one.

Dave moved over to clean up the broken mugs and tea. Why did she do that? He'd thought that she might have enjoyed the kiss but was too embarrassed to say anything. He had felt the chemistry between them at work, so if she felt the same way about him, why was she acting so strange? Come to think of it, she'd been acting funny since she came out of hospital. Maybe he should leave. Maybe he had misread her feelings for him. No, he couldn't leave her in this state. He had to find out what was wrong with her. He had to know why her feelings had changed so much in just a couple of months. He decided to go up to her room and find out just what the hell was going on.

Emma lay on her bed face down, thinking. She really liked Dave, she even thought that she might be able to love him but she was so scared. She didn't want him to get hurt and that was exactly what would happen if HE found out the truth about why she'd been in hospital. Dave would never want her then. And as for a physical relationship, she didn't think she could ever have sex again without thinking about that man. Just look what a simple kiss had triggered off. Was everything going to remind her of what had happened? Would she ever be able to forget and live a normal life? She heard the door creak open and turned to look towards it.

Dave came in and sat down on the edge of the bed. Looking at Emma he said, "Emma, I want to know the truth. The truth about why you were in hospital? The truth about why you are limping? And the truth about why you've had all those new locks put on the door? But most of all I want to know why your feelings have suddenly changed towards me? We used to laugh and flirt together and there definitely was something there. If you want to be just friends that's fine with me but you've shut me out and I can't understand why?"

She turned away, unable to keep the tears from streaming down her face. "I can't tell you Dave."

"Emma, I care for you, please tell me what's going on? Please."

"Just leave Dave, I can't tell you." Emma turned away from him, hoping he would just leave but instead Dave put his arm around her.

"Please tell me." He said in a soothing voice.

Emma looked straight at him, her eyes full of tears, "Ok," she said, "You know that story in the paper two months ago about the victim who got away from the Rosehill Rapist?"

"Yes, I can't believe that the police haven't caught him yet. I know that girl must be scared but she should be able to help them enough to catch him, I would have thought."

"That was me!" Emma interrupted.

"What?" Dave said, unbelieving.

"That was me!" She repeated "I'm the one that got away."

He sat there stunned. He didn't know what to do or say. It was so shocking. He'd imagined all sorts of things but never this. He wished that he could take the hurt out of her eyes, the hurt out of her life. He pulled her to him and held her tightly. Placing a kiss delicately on her forehead he asked, "Why the hell didn't you tell me?"

"I didn't know how you felt about me. I liked you a lot and I didn't want to spoil our friendship. I don't think a lot of myself at the moment, and I thought that if I told anyone, that they wouldn't like me much either."

"Why should I think like that? Why should anyone think like

that, it wasn't your fault?"

"I know that now but I thought you might think it was. At first, I thought that it was entirely my fault, I felt dirty and cheap; I thought that everyone else would think the same way, until Jackie managed to stop me thinking like that. Now I just feel so small that I just want to hide away and never see anyone."

They sat there on the bed talking for ages about lots of things, including how they felt about each other.

"I can't think about a relationship right now. You understand, it's not you Dave, it's me." Emma explained. "I need friends more than anything."

"I understand, I'll be there for you and if you ever change your mind, you let me know." Dave pulled her to him, kissing her on the forehead and holding her tight. Still a little upset, Emma fell asleep in his arms, which left Dave thinking. He'd wait for her; he'd always wait for her.

After Dave was sure that Emma had fallen into a deep enough sleep he wriggled himself out from under her. Leaving her sleeping in bed he decided to nip down the road to the local Chinese and get some food. It had been a long day and he hadn't had anything to eat since breakfast. Plus, Emma needed something to keep her strength up. He'd let her sleep now, God knows she needed it and he'd wake her when he got back. He took her keys and headed off down the road.

He stood in the shadows of the alley across from Emma's house. It was his favourite place to watch from. Under the cover of darkness, he could see everything and no one could see him. With the light on in the bedroom and the curtains open, he could see her lying on the bed. It was the only light on in the entire house. She was such a slut. He was going to make her suffer for this. She was going to pay. He left the alley and headed up the road.

Just then the phone rang, waking Emma up from her slumber. She looked around the room, Dave must have gone downstairs, she thought. Emma quickly picked the receiver it up.

"You slut!" The harsh voice shouted some more foul names down the phone at her and then he said, "You'll pay for this. Just you wait and see." Then the line went quiet as he put the receiver down.

The phone rang again, despite being scared to pick it up, she did. "Why can't you just leave me alone?" She shouted down the line.

"Easy, its Steve, I take it you had another call from him?"

"Yes, did you trace it?"

"Unfortunately, the call was too quick. How are you feeling?"

"Apart from frightened, I'm fine." Emma looked at the clock and saw it was 9pm. "Oh...and the cat's still smiling." She added, knowing that deep down inside it wasn't really.

"Okay, I'm glad you remembered that bit. Oh, who was that man with you tonight?" He said, trying to keep the jealously out of his voice.

"It was Dave that friend from the bar I told you about. He's just keeping me company. I feel better with someone around."

"Okay but next time you've got someone we haven't seen before coming round you need to let us know. I'll call you at the usual time tomorrow. Bye!" He said, thinking that he should be the one who's keeping her company and not Dave!

She put the receiver down. Steve was a bit short with her. She wondered why. Maybe he was having a bad day at work.

Just then Emma heard the front door opening. She got off the bed and crept to the top of the stairs to see who it was. As she reached the top of the stairs she could hear plates and cutlery being moved around in the kitchen. Her heart was pounding so hard that it felt like it was going to break through her chest cavity.

Tip-toeing down the stairs, she walked to the kitchen door and peered round the doorframe. She breathed a huge sigh of relief. It was only Dave.

"Good to see your awake, I took your keys and went to get food. Hope you like Chinese?"

Chapter Eleven

Steve sat in his office chewing the end of his pen; his chair swivelled round to look out the window instead of facing the picture board of all the Rosehill Rapists victims. He was mainly facing that way so he didn't have to look at the picture of Emma that was up there.

He'd watched the sunrise light up the sky with its oranges, yellows and pinks, filling him full of warmth. Sunrise was his favourite part of the day. Steve found it so relaxing to watch how each morning entered the world more beautiful than the last. Steve just wished he had a better place than his office to watch it from. He visualized a picturesque seaside house with a huge bay window, which lead from the bedroom onto a terrace where he would sit watching the sunrise while enjoying his coffee and croissants. And who better to enjoy it all with than Emma, the only thing more beautiful than the sunrise itself. There she was, back in his head again.

He'd been trying not to think about her since he'd phoned her last night. In fact he'd been trying to think of her as the victim and not as the attractive beautiful woman he wanted since he'd phoned her a few weeks back when her *friend* Dave had been there. Unsuccessfully, his brain wouldn't stop and he was flitting constantly between wonderful daydreams and fighting the green-eyed monster since he'd found out about Dave.

Emma was most likely asleep in bed now. Probably with Dave lying beside her, holding her in his arms. He hated that thought. If only he had met her first. If only he didn't have to play the tough Detective, she might feel the same way he did. He wished that he were with her today. He would drive her out to the country, away from all this hustle and bustle; they'd have a picnic. It would be wonderful if only it could happen. Well, there was no harm in dreaming. Except the fact that it made you feel so damn miserable knowing that you couldn't do anything about it!

There was a knock on the door, bringing him out of his daydream. Angry and disappointed, he swivelled his chair back round to his desk and yelled, "Come in."

Colin's face appeared at the door. "There's been another murder!" He said.

Steve grabbed his coat and headed for the door. "Any idea who it is yet?"

"No, not yet, Sir."

"Where is it?"

"Melrose Gardens. Don't know how he managed it Sir, they've got a neighbourhood watch scheme going on but no one saw a thing."

"Neighbourhood watch is only for nosy neighbours who've got nothing better to do with their time than spread gossip. Obviously the nosy ones are away on holiday." He headed out the door to his car. Melrose Gardens, Why did that rang a bell?

While driving out there, he wondered why the murderer had chosen Melrose Gardens to do his next grisly murder. It was miles away from the rest.

As he turned off Aberdeen Way into Melrose Gardens, he realized why he'd recognized the name; he'd been out here with Mary before. She had some stuck up friends out this way. It was that dinner party with the Catterwells. He remembered now, how they'd left half way through dinner. Of course, it was entirely his fault. If he remembered rightly it was something about jobs.

Mary had brought up how she didn't like him working in the police force. The husband had offered him a job with his company. It was like she'd planned for all it to happen. He knew how she felt but he loved his job. He'd trained for years to get where he was today and he wasn't going to give it up just like that. Mary couldn't understand it, she never would. They then began arguing, and he'd dragged her home. A great end to an equally great dinner party! And that was start of their break up.

As he drove through the blockade of police cars he could see the body. A large blanket covered it. Obviously one of the residents who had found it had covered it over.

He got out of his car and walked over to it. One of the officers joined him. "She's in a bad way Sir. No fingers, no teeth, and she's been cut about a bit, especially on the face. I've kept all the neighbours away. The only one who's seen her is Mr Pentney.

He was packing his car, getting ready to go on holiday with his family."

As Steve pulled back the blanket his heart leapt into his throat. He couldn't believe it, it was Mary. His Mary. He wasn't expecting that one! He felt like he'd taken a bullet to the chest. Why Mary? Why of all people did it have to be Mary? His legs were trembling. He backed up, away from the body to his car and leant against it. He looked up the road. There was her car. The battered, blue Ford Escort that he'd bought Mary as her first car. He'd spent so much money in repairs because it meant so much to her and had tried but had never been able to get her trade it in for a newer model. Why hadn't he noticed it when he pulled up? What was she doing here? Where were the boys? He had to see his boys.

"What's wrong sir?" The young officer said. "You look like you've seen a ghost?"

"That's my ex-wife." Steve said, fighting back the tears trying to break through he turned and looked up the street. "Look I've got to find out where my boys are. I've got to see if they're all right. Call Detective Nick Fisher to do the paperwork on this one. He's been helping on the case; he'll know what to do. I'll look at it when he's finished. Tell him we've got a positive I.D. on it and I already know who it is. Tell him who it is and he'll understand. Also, that Escort over there is hers. Have it shipped to the station, and give it a good going over. I'll catch you at the station later."

He got in his car, drove over to Mary's house. He rang the doorbell but there was no answer. Then he realized this was the weekend the boys were at his mother's. He'd been so wrapped up with his work he'd forgotten that he was supposed to be over there for Sunday lunch. Well he wouldn't miss it but he didn't think he'd want it either. He started the car and drove off.

As he headed up St Johns Road and parked his car he wondered how the hell he was going to tell his boys what had happened to their mum. He walked up to the front door and rang the bell. His mum had given him a spare key but, as always, it was in his kitchen drawer at home. As he stood in the porch waiting for his mum to come to the door he noticed the curtains were pulled back in the lounge and two cheeky faces appeared in the gap laughing and waving frantically at him. Steve could see that they were still in their pyjamas, probably sitting there watching early morning cartoons. "Get up Gran! Dad's here!" They shouted, so happy to see him and here he was about to ruin their day.

He could see his mum through the frosted glass of the front door slowly descending the stairs in her dressing gown and slippers.

"You're here early love?" His mum said as she opened the front door looking puzzled because he was always late for Sunday lunch. She had started telling him that lunch would be at midday and serving it a two because he could never turn up on time. Then she noticed that he was upset about something. "I'll go and put the kettle on."

His mum headed down the hallway to the kitchen leaving the hall space completely clear and, using it like a runway, the boys darted up it and nearly knocked him to the floor while flinging their arms round him. They started talking in unison about totally different things, stuff that had happened at school that week and what that they had been doing with their mum. They sounded like the characters from the Alvin & The Chipmunks cartoon that they liked to watch on TV. It was hard to understand what either of them was saying at the best of times, let alone now. "Okay! Okay!" Steve said, trying hard not to show his real feelings. "We'll talk about all of this in a moment. Can you go and get yourselves dressed, your Gran and I have something to discuss."

"Okay Dad." They said, again in unison, and together they ran upstairs. He watched them go upstairs shouting, "Make sure you wash and brush those teeth." They were only seven and eight. Scott, the eight year old, had been a difficult birth. It seemed like hours before he'd come into the world. Ross was a lot easier, one push and he was there or so it had seemed. Mary had told him that it was a lot harder than it looked. Steve swallowed and took a deep breath in to control his emotions. They might have been divorced but he still loved Mary and that made what he had to do even harder. He hadn't even had time to come to terms with what had happened himself yet.

Steve sighed. He really wished that he didn't have to tell them. He wished that Mary would come through the door and say that it was all a joke to try and get him to give up his job. He wished it would go away or that he'd wake up and it would just be a dream.

"What's wrong dear?" His Mum said, waking him from his thoughts. She wasn't a typical grey-haired granny. She had her hair in a short, cropped style, wore jeans and sweaters, and had more life than he could ever imagine which was a good job really because she was going to need it. Although she was sixty-four, she acted like seventeen sometimes. He was proud to have her as his Mum, and grateful too.

Steve followed her into the sitting room and as she placed the cups of tea on the living room table he said, "You'd better sit down for this." Slumping down into the armchair that used to be his dad's before he died that had now become his when he visited and placing his hands to his head he tried to think of how to word what he needed to tell his mum.

She could see by the way he'd slumped down into the armchair that he'd had the stuffing knocked out of him. She looked at him quizzically.

"Mum, this is very hard for me, I've only just found out but I really don't know how else to word it. I had a call this morning and it's Mary, she's been killed."

"Oh Lord! Was anyone else hurt?"

"No, Mum, it wasn't an accident. She was.." There wasn't any way else he could put it. "She was murdered."

"Oh no, dear God no!" She said as the tears started to fall. She reached inside her dressing gown pocket for her hanky. "Are you sure?"

"I didn't know it was her until I got there mum, it was awful. I didn't want to believe it was her but it was. It was definitely her." He started to feel tears escaping and sniffed back the build up in his nostrils. There came a loud thud from upstairs bringing them both back to reality and the biggest problem that was now facing them. How to tell the boys, who were upstairs fighting by the sounds of it, about their mum's death?

"What are you going to tell the boys?" She asked. "You can't tell them the truth Steve, they'll never understand it."

"It's all right mum, I think I've got it covered. I'll tell them that she was involved in a car accident, at least until they are both old enough to understand. I can't think of any reason that they should know any different at the moment. I need to protect them and if lying is the only way to do it then that's what I am going to have to do." Steve never did like lying. Mary and him had always made a point of punishing the boys when they did but what could he do in this instance.

He got up, wiped the tears off his face and walked over to his mum. Sitting beside her on the sofa, he held her in his arms. "I need your help on this one, mum. You've got to be strong for me and strong for the boys too. They're going to need you; this is going to be so hard on them. You're the only grandparent left since

Mary's Dad died last year and they were upset enough when that happened."

"They can come and live with me, Steve. Don't you worry I'll be there for them. This is the best place for them." She said mopping up her tears with her slightly soggy hanky. "You've got a very important job, even more important now. I want you to understand that they'll not be a burden here. You just make sure you catch the animal that did this to our Mary."

They had talked about this before Mary's Dad had died and they had come to the decision then that if anything had happened to Mary or to the both of them then the boys would go and live with his Mum so that Steve could keep working. She was a lot healthier than Mary's Dad and didn't live that far from Steve's flat or the police station.

He wiped the fresh tears from his eyes and took a deep breath in. This was going to be hard. "I'll call them down, there's no reason to put it off." Steve opened the door to the living room and yelled up the stairs, "Scott! Ross! Can you come down please I've got to tell you something!"

They came thundering down the stairs. They sounded a lot like a herd of elephants. Ross was first into the sitting room and sat straight on his Dad's lap. "Dad! Scott said that if I don't do as he says the bogey man will get me. He won't get me, will he Dad?"

"No Ross, he won't get you because there is no such thing as the bogey man." He wished he could be sure of what he was telling Ross but after what had been happening, he was beginning to wonder. "Okay boys," Steve said, putting his arms round them. "I need you to be quiet for a minute I've got something important to tell you."

"Why are you crying Gran?" Scott asked.

"Listen to your Dad." She said through the sniffles and looking away from the boys she reached over for a tissue to replace her worn out hanky.

"Boys, it's your Mum. She's had an accident."

"Is she all right?" Scott asked, pulling out from under Steve's arm and looking him the eyes.

"I'm afraid she isn't son. She's...erm." How the hell could he put it? "She's...She's gone to heaven to be with granddad. It was a very bad accident. They tried to help her but there wasn't anything that anyone could do."

Ross started to sniffle, and trying to understand what his dad was saying, Scott asked, "Does that mean she'll be back to pick us up tomorrow instead of today?"

"I'm afraid not." Steve said, "Now that she's with granddad in heaven she can't come back. You're going live here with Gran now and I will come over and see you every day."

Steve pulled Scott to him and hugged the both of them as tight as he could. It was no use, he couldn't stop the tears from falling, and as his Mum joined in the hug it was even more impossible to stop the tears.

Yet, unbelievably, through all of this his mind wandered off track and he thought of Emma.

Emma felt relieved that she'd spoken to Dave. It was like a great weight had been lifted off her shoulders. Even Jackie said that she had noticed that she seemed a lot happier, and having Dave call round to see how they were made them both feel that little bit safer.

Emma still had her quiet moments though, generally after one of the phone calls, and while in these moods she liked to disappear upstairs and hide away from everyone. Emma always did her best never to cry in front of anyone, and upstairs was the best place to be when this was going to happen. Nobody could see her there.

Emma still couldn't understand why this had happened to her? The worst thing was that she had involved Jackie and now Dave. She hadn't really wanted to involve anyone but it had just happened.

Emma had needed Jackie around though; it would have been awful living alone and having to deal with everything that was going on. She would have been going out of her mind by now, with the thoughts of what had happened, so she was glad to have her best friend around if only to keep putting her straight.

Also, she would have gone completely mad waiting for the phone to ring, and even madder still when it did eventually ring if Jackie wasn't there to answer it occasionally. Even now she was on edge, jumping each time it rang. At least she knew that three times a day it would be Steve calling to check up on her and she'd try to keep him chatting on the line to avoid any other calls coming through. Talking of calls, he hadn't called her today to check up? It was eleven-thirty and she hadn't heard a peep.

Steve. Now there was a strange man. He'd come round quite often since she'd made a full statement, and she didn't think that it was just to make sure she was okay. They'd spend many hours chatting when Dave wasn't there but then if he was there, Steve would only have a coffee and then go. Sometimes he didn't even have a coffee. Anybody would think that he had a crush on her, the way he was acting but he couldn't have, could he?

He was a very handsome man, and she did find herself attracted to him but she had Dave.

Dave was so patient and kind. He understood that she just needed friends around at the moment. Anyway, she was probably imagining things. How could Steve like her? He probably fancied Jackie. Come to think of it, he'd always asked if Jackie was home when he came round.

Jackie and Dave were both at work today. Dave was working all today and Jackie was working until three. Sundays were always like that. Especially since Geoff had started doing Sunday roasts.

Emma often wished that she hadn't handed in her notice and when she'd spoken to Steve last time she'd mentioned she was thinking of asking for her old job back but he had advised her not to do so just yet. At least if Emma was at work she'd have something to keep her mind off the rape and *HIM*. She was so bored at home. There's only so many times you clean the house and even that didn't stop her thinking about the rape. Even when she was deeply engrossed in a book or film she found that her mind wandered off back to the bloody subject. It wasn't fair.

The phone didn't ring as much as it used to but she'd always find herself looking forward to Steve's calls three times a day and dreading the phone the rest of the day. More often than not Emma found herself wishing that Steve would pop round and keep her company whilst Jackie and Dave were at work. While in the midst of this thought, there came a knock at the door.

She looked through the peephole. It was Steve, well, what a coincidence. She opened the door, greeting him with a big grin, "Talk of the devil and he shall appear. I was just...thinking...about you..." And then she noticed that he didn't look at all happy.

"What's wrong?" She asked. She'd never seen him this down before.

"There's been another murder." He walked past her and into the kitchen.

"Do you want a drink?" Emma asked, feeling a responsible pang of guilt pass through her like a cold chill. "You look as if you could do with a strong one?"

"Have you got any whisky? A very large one would be good!" He asked, sitting down at the kitchen table.

"Sure, I think I might have one myself." She stated.

There was a short spell of silence as she poured the drinks and sat down. And then she asked, "Was it him?" like she didn't know already what the answer would be.

"Yes, it was him. The white rose was left there as his calling card." Steve said sullenly.

"Do you know who it is yet?" Emma asked.

"Yes. It's my ex-wife." He just stared blankly into space.

Now she was puzzled. He hadn't told her that he was previously married. Not that he had to tell her. They'd had many conversations but this had never cropped up. She didn't know what to say, so she got up, walked round the table, stood behind him and put her arms round his neck.

Steve couldn't believe what she had just done but he didn't say anything because it felt so damn good. He just gave a big sigh and closed his eyes. He wished that she would hold him like this all afternoon. Mind you she was a cuddly person and this was probably normal for her and meant nothing more than a friendly hug but being in her arms meant everything to him at the moment and his problems seemed to just disappear. It was just like paradise, which came to an abrupt end, like someone dragging the needle across a record to stop it playing, as Jackie walked into the kitchen.

Shocked by what she'd walking in on, Jackie asked, "Emma, can you and I have a word in private please?"

"I'll be back in a minute." Emma said, and followed Jackie upstairs to her room.

Jackie shut the door behind them. "What the hell is going on?"

"Nothing!"

"What! You had your arms round him. Don't tell me nothing's going on. What's Dave going to say?"

Emma decided to keep her true feelings out of this one. "Jackie, the man's just lost his ex-wife for Christ sakes. I didn't know what to say to him, so I just gave him a hug. Besides Dave and I are only friends, I know he wants more but I can't be sure what I want at the moment."

Jackie looked apologetic. "I'm sorry." She said, "I just jumped to conclusions. I shouldn't have done that."

"That's okay!" Emma said. "I'm going back down now. Could you leave us alone for a while?"

"Sure, no problem."

Emma shut the door behind her and infuriated at her friend's outburst she went back down to the kitchen. Steve was sat slouched in the chair, swirling his drink around in the glass. She went over and picked hers up, and drank it down in one large gulp. Steve followed suit.

"Why don't you stay and have something to eat?" Emma said, wanting deep down in her heart for him to do so.

"Sorry, I can't." He said, wishing he could. "I've got to go to my Mums for tea. She's got the boys, and I really should be with them."

The boys, she thought, he's got kids as well? How many? "That's okay, maybe some other time then." Clearly there was a lot she didn't know about Steve Harris.

He could see disappointment mixed with confusion in her eyes so he said, "Tell you what I'll come round after I've put the boys to bed. It'll be about nine. Is that okay?"

"That'll be fine, I've been having a little trouble sleeping anyway so don't worry about keeping me up. We'll have a real good chat."

Chapter Twelve

It was nearly ten when Steve eventually knocked on the door. The house was getting unbearably quiet by that time. Jackie had gone out to meet up with Tony for their date and had told Emma not to wait up. Dave was working a double shift so had said he would pop by late afternoon tomorrow, so Emma had eventually sat there watching but not watching, TV. She hated being on her own with her thoughts. At first she'd tried reading but couldn't concentrate on her book then she'd turned on the stereo and sat there still unable to switch off her thoughts, then after going stir crazy for a while she'd given up on music and turned on the TV.

He hadn't rung today; maybe he'd decided to give up on his little game of cat and mouse. He had committed another murder, could it be possible he didn't want to carry on playing with her anymore. She wished deep down inside that it were true. It would be a great relief to be able to get on with life again. To be able to leave the house without the worry of whether he would be around the next corner waiting for her.

Sometimes Emma felt like screaming out so loud that she would break every pane of glass in her windows. She dreamt of getting out of the house, going to the beach and feeling the salty air on her face. Maybe she could get a house by the beach, change her name and assume a new life like they did in the movies. Emma wanted to be able to enjoy life, to feel free again.

Anyway, she was glad when Steve eventually turned up. Emma peered through the peephole. It was Steve all right, and he had a bag in one hand that was labelled "Thresher's". He was obviously planning on drowning his sorrows tonight. Emma didn't blame him either and she certainly wasn't going to say 'no' to drowning with him.

She opened the door. "Come on in." Emma said.

"I hope you don't mind but I brought us some drink. Thought we might get drunk, we've both got a good excuse." He wandered into the sitting room. "Jackie not here?" He asked.

It was more of a statement than a question but she answered him anyway. "No, she's gone out with Tony."

"Well, it looks like it's just you and me kid! Talking of kids, I'm sorry I'm late, it took me ages to get the boys to bed."

"It's okay I can understand how upset they must be. Have a seat, I'll go and get us some glasses and some ice." She went into the kitchen, stopping on the way to check her reflection in the mirror. She didn't know why she did, he'd made it plainly obvious that he fancied Jackie, he even seemed disappointed when he found out she wasn't there.

When she went back in he'd sat himself down by the window. He looked so lonely in his thoughts.

"Thinking about your boys?" She asked.

"Yeah, I feel bad because I couldn't bring myself to tell them the truth. I told them that their mother had been involved in an accident. I've never lied to them before." He stared out of the window again.

"It's okay Steve. When they're older they'll understand that you only lied to protect them." Emma said as she filled two tumblers with the whiskey that he'd brought over. The ice starting cracking immediately as the warm liquid made its way round them.

This only highlighted the fact of how quiet it was in the room.

Steve reached over picked up one of the glasses and drank it straight down.

"Want another?" Emma said, already knowing what his answer would be.

Steve nodded. "If I ever catch that bastard I'm going to string him up! I'll make him pay for this!" He swallowed the second glass just as quickly, placed it back on the table and put his head in his hands.

Emma got up off her chair and went over and knelt down in front of him. She put her arms around him. Emma could feel him trembling in her grasp, so she held him tighter. They remained like that for what seemed like an eternity then Steve lifted his head and said, "Thanks." And before she knew it he was kissing her.

Emma quickly pulled away. Not because it didn't feel good, it was quite the opposite, it felt very good. She pulled away because she knew it was wrong. Very wrong but very right! She had already told Dave that she wasn't ready for a relationship at the moment, and Emma thought she wasn't but now she was more confused than ever.

"I'm sorry," Steve said, "I shouldn't have done that. I'd better go." He stood and grabbed his coat off the back of the chair.

"It's okay." Emma said. "Don't be so silly. Things like that happen. You've had a hard day and you're confused and exhausted. We'll forget it ever happened. Besides, you can't go you've had too much to drink. We can't have a drunk detective on the roads can we now."

"I've only had two."

"Yeah, two really large whiskeys, definitely more than a double shot each, I think that makes you over the limit even if you aren't drunk and I should know I used to work in a bar."

"No I really should be going. I'll call a taxi or get a bus or something."

"Look, I've got a sofa bed, and it is surprisingly comfortable. Why don't we just get unbelievably drunk, you can spend the night and I'll do a fried breakfast for you in the morning? Build up your strength so you can go out and catch a killer." Emma said smiling and trying to diffuse the situation, hoping deep down inside that Steve would stay. "Besides, truth is, I could really do with the company. I'm going loopy just sat here all the time."

How could he refuse an offer like that? The icing on the cake would be for her to join him on the sofa bed but he'd just found out that would never happen. Looking into her eyes, he knew that Emma just wanted someone to stay with her and it was just for the company and nothing more. Had she told Dave this too or was Emma more than just friends with him? Anyway, if she was willing to forget, then so was he, besides he could do with some friendly company at the moment too. He slumped back down in the chair.

"Tell me about your boys." Emma said, changing the subject. Emma noticed how his face changed, when she mentioned them. She could see he was very proud of them and loved them a lot. It made her sad to think that they had lost their mother and the guilt came back. Maybe if she had told the police a bit sooner, then Mary might never have been murdered. Or had he found out that she had told the police and that's why Mary got murdered?

When Dave pulled up outside he noticed the sitting room light highlighting a crack in the drawn curtains.

"Good she's still up." Dave said to himself and got out of the car and headed up the steps to the front door. He'd knocked on the door but no one answered. It wasn't like Emma to leave her living room light on. Worried, Dave stepped over the small border hedge onto the front lawn and peered through a gap in the curtains that hung at the window. Emma was lying, curled up on the sofa sound asleep while in the arm chair by the window was Steve, head lolled forward, with a glass still in his hand. Looking on the table, Dave noticed two empty bottles of Jack Daniels and a second glass. It seemed that Emma and Steve were both as dead as the bottles of Jack Daniels. Obviously they'd had a good night, he thought. He walked back to his car with the green-eyed monster in tow.

As Dave drove home, he couldn't help but think that something was going on between them. He kept telling this thought to get out of his head but, like a boomerang, it kept on coming back. When he got home he went straight to bed and when he did eventually get to sleep, his dreams were filled with pictures of the two of them kissing each other.

Jackie crept in at three in the morning. She'd had a great night with Tony. He'd taken her back to his flat and they'd had a very cosy nightcap. It was a shame she'd had to leave but Jackie promised him that next time they went out she'd stay a whole weekend with him. Jackie didn't tell him but she just needed to speak to Emma first and make sure that she was ok with it. Emma had been very clingy just lately but Jackie could understand her not wanting to be on her own.

As Jackie entered the hallway she wondered why Emma had left the light on in the lounge. She opened the door and reached in to switch it off. As she did she noticed Emma sleeping on the sofa.

I knew she'd wait up for me, Jackie thought. I'd better wake her or she'll be stiff in the morning.

Jackie was just about to lean over and shake Emma awake when she noticed Steve slouched in the armchair by the window and decided to leave her after all. Switching off the light, Jackie went to bed.

Chapter Thirteen

Emma awoke the next morning feeling extremely groggy. At first she didn't realize where she was. Her neck was stiff and her head was throbbing. Why wasn't she in bed? Looking over towards the window she saw Steve slouched in the armchair, glass still in hand. Then she remembered; what a night!

It was like they were old friends that hadn't seen each other for years, catching up on each other's news. They'd talked about everything, once the shock of the kiss had been forgotten, of course. Steve talked more about his boys, then about his marriage and his job. Emma had told him about how she'd come to live in Ipswich because of her parents.

They then talked about music, films, likes and dislikes.

Emma couldn't believe the amount of things she and Steve had in common. They had some thought-provoking moments and, once the drink kicked in, some extremely silly ones. "Oh god!" She said quietly to herself as she suddenly remembered something she now wished she hadn't done.

"Have you got a middle name?" She'd asked Steve loudly. She'd always gotten loud when she was drunk.

"Yes but I'm not telling you it!" He'd replied with a drunken slur.

"I'll tell you mine if you tell me yours!" She'd goaded him.

"No way!"

Emma had then moved across the room to his chair, started tickling him under the arms and yelling, "Tell me! Tell me!" until he'd eventually given in.

"Ok already, I'll tell you. Mine's Robert. Stephen Robert Harris. See it's a horrible name and I hate it."

"Well I like it Mr Stephen Robert Harris. Detective Superintendent Stephen Robert Harris. I like that a lot." She'd said cheekily grinning from ear to ear like a Cheshire cat.

"Come on then, tell me yours."

"No way!" She'd said and ran, well hobbled as fast as she could back over to the sofa.

"Well, I guess it's your turn then!" He'd said as he started to get his own back by tickling her.

"Stop it Steve!" She'd yelled between giggles.

"Tell me then. Fair's fair."

"Ok, it's Jane. Plain Jane."

"Well I don't think it's plain. I think that it's very nice. Miss Emma Jane Parker." He'd said.

"Stop it, you remind me of my father. When I'd been a bad girl he'd shout 'Miss Emma Jane Parker you get to your room!' I'd always know I was in deep trouble when he said my full name."

"So Miss Emma Jane Parker, you've been a naughty girl then!" Steve had then moved in closer. "Maybe I should arrest you."

Emma could remember feeling her breath shortening as her heart began to race and looking him straight in the eyes she'd said, "You don't need to arrest me, I'm a very good girl now." And with that she'd leant over and quickly kissed him cheekily on the lips.

Emma then remembered how Steve had grabbed her waist and pulling her tightly to him, kissing first her lips then down one side of her neck, nibbling her ear lobe as he past it by. Emma remembered moaning with pleasure as he pushed her top down her shoulder and gently bit the warm bare flesh.

Oh God what had she done? Emma thought as she got up off the sofa her head pounded like the bass on a full volume speaker. Emma hoped with all her heart that he didn't remember what had happened last night and she headed to the kitchen for a glass of water and some aspirin.

"Good morning!" Jackie sang as Emma entered the kitchen.

"Shhh, not so loud ok!" Emma whispered.

"Somebody have a good evening with Mr J D last night then?" Jackie giggled.

"That somebody has got a very thick head because of excessive amounts of Mr J D but you need to be quiet because Mr S H is still sleeping. Have you had any breakfast?"

"Not yet, why?" Jackie asked.

"I thought I'd do us a fry-up."

"That sounds great."

"Good. Would you mind going down the shop to get some eggs and bacon while I take a shower and try to get rid of this head?" Emma asked, downing a couple of aspirin.

"No, not at all but you're paying." Jackie laughed.

"There's a ten pound note in my purse." Emma said through a yawn and headed up stairs.

Steve woke up to the sound of a hairdryer and a man drumming the inside his head. He had definitely had too much drink last night. Standing up and stretching he rolled his neck to one side then the other, feeling it click as he did so. He wandered into the kitchen and grabbed a glass of water, downing it to take the taste of stale whiskey from his mouth.

Steve put the kettle on and headed upstairs to relieve himself of the excessive amount of liquid he'd drunk last night. As he headed to the bathroom he looked across the hall to the room where the noise of the hairdryer was coming from.

The door was slightly ajar and he could see Emma patiently pulling a brush through her hair with one hand as she waved the dryer at it with the other. Her hair had a lustrous sheen as it caught the light from the nearby window. Mesmerized he followed her hair down her back to her slender waistline where little black lace panties hugged the perfectly smooth skin of her slender hips.

Steve thought about the kiss last night and wished he'd have pushed her just that little bit further. Who knows he could have been waking up next to that gorgeous body this morning instead of in the armchair with everyone's best friend, Harry Hangover.

He'd had a great time last night. It was like they'd been friends for years but Steve knew it could be more. Something was bubbling under the surface that could lead to better and stronger things. There was definitely some kind of chemistry there but he didn't want to push it in case he scared Emma off. She'd been through so much and he knew that putting her on the spot wouldn't be the way to go. He'd just have to take his time.

Shit! Steve thought as the memories of a second more passionate embrace flooded his mind. It seemed he was closer to waking up to her than he'd thought. Luckily though she'd passed out before they'd gotten too carried away with the moment, which also that she probably didn't remember what had happened, he hoped.

If they hadn't have been drunk Steve could believe that it would lead to something more and boy, did he want to lead to more. Emma had smelt so good when he was kissing her, a kind of warm, cosy smell that seemed to lure him in and make him feel the need to take her so much. If Emma hadn't of passed out then Steve doubted that in the state he was in that he would have been able to stop himself.

Brought back to reality by a key unlocking the front door Steve hurried into the bathroom. Luckily someone had left a towel in there so he proceeded to take a cold shower followed by a hot one.

On leaving the bathroom Steve was greeted by the heavenly smell of bacon and freshly brewed coffee and headed down to the kitchen.

"Good morning ladies." Steve said as he entered the kitchen, pretending that nothing had happened last night. "Certainly, smells good in here. How long before breakfast is ready?"

"Oh...about 10 minutes I reckon." Emma replied, relieved to find that Steve didn't seem to remember much about last night.

"Is it all right if I give the boys a call?" Steve asked.

"Yeah sure, use the phone in the hall." Emma replied.

Jackie waited patiently until Steve had disappeared into the hallway closing the door behind him before saying. "You sure look comfy with each other today. Have a good night last night, did we?"

"Well we had a good drink if that's what you mean." Emma said, hoping that Jackie couldn't sense that something *had* happened last night.

"Look if some kind of relationship is growing between you and Steve then good for you but I don't want to see you leading Dave on at the same time. Dave's been a good mate to me since I moved to Ipswich and I don't want to see him hurt. He's got quite a thing for you."

"Nothing is happening between me and either of them Jackie." Emma lied. "Steve and I just had a good chat and a good drink last night. God knows we both needed it."

"Well you both look like you enjoyed it too!" Jackie said, sensing her friend was hiding something.

"Jackie, give me a break will you. I'm not ready for anything with anyone. Please get it into your thick skull." Emma said, turning away and plating up the bacon and eggs.

"I'm sorry Emma." Jackie said, wishing she'd never brought it up. She didn't want to upset Emma but she had to make sure that Emma wouldn't be hurt again. "You know me, just an old worrywart."

"How are you holding up?" Steve's mum asked him.

"Not too bad. I had a long chat with a friend last night." Steve could hear the girls talking as he was on the phone to his mum but he couldn't quite make-out what the conversation was about. "How are the boys? Are they behaving?" He asked, slightly distracted, trying to move closer to the door to hear what they were saying.

"They missed you when they got up. We had a few tears this morning but I don't think it's hit them properly yet. Are you going into work today?"

"Not today mum. I'm going to phone in and request a couple of days off to spend with the boys."

"Good, they could do with you around for a few days. What time will I see you?"

"About dinnertime, I've just got to nip into work and pick up a couple of things." Steve lied, not wanting his mum to know that he had spent the night round Emma's house, getting drunk. "Got to go, see you around dinnertime."

"See you later on then." His mum said and hung up.

Steve leant in closer to the kitchen door but whatever the subject was that Emma and Jackie had been talking about was now finished and they were talking about Jackie's relationship with Tony. Damn, I bet she's told Jackie everything. He wished he knew what she remembered.

Steve picked up the receiver again and dialled the office.

"I'm glad you called." Bill started. Steve knew where he was going before Bill finished his sentence. The tone of his voice was a dead giveaway. "I think you need to take some time off so I'm taking you off the case."

"You can't do that Bill! I've put a lot of man-hours into this case! You can't take me off it now!"

"I know you've worked hard on it Steve but I think you've become too emotionally involved. I'm putting Nick Fisher in charge. He's been working with you on this so he knows what's happening."

"Nick Fisher can't handle this case! It's too big for him. Look I only need a couple of days off to spend with the boys. Hell, I'll even take the files home with me and do some work at home."

"Look, I'm putting you on a month's leave to sort out your boys and anything else that's possibly playing on your mind at the moment."

"What the hell are you talking about Bill?"

"I know you spent last night round the victim's house, Steve. You've been spending a lot of time round there of late and I think it's clouding your vision. There, I've said it. I didn't want to go there but you made me."

"We're just friends and that's got nothing to do with my work! I've put everything I've got into this case. Nick Fisher will never catch him. You take me off it then you'll be making a big mistake!"

"I don't want any more arguments off you Steve. You're taking the time off and that's that. Oh and next time your planning on being 'just friends', close the damn curtains properly! The boys got quite a show last night."

Steve angrily slammed the phone down. "Shit!" They'd seen everything. Thank God Emma had passed out. The show might have been a lot more exciting for them if she hadn't. He headed back to the kitchen.

"How are the boys coping?" Emma asked as Steve walked back into the kitchen with an air of anger around him.

"The boys are fine," Steve replied.

Noticing Steve was angry Emma asked, "What's up?"

"You aren't going to believe this. I called the Super to ask for a couple of days off to be with the boys and he's taking me off the case."

"Why?" Emma asked, trying not to show how disappointed she was.

"He says that I'm too personally involved. He mentioned that I've been spending too much time round here and he seems to think that it's affecting my work." He angrily stabbed at a piece of bacon with his fork.

Jackie looked from Steve to Emma and back to Steve again, her eyes widening as she did so.

"I told him we were just friends but for some reason he didn't believe me." Steve looked at Emma's face to see if he could get some reaction to that statement but she just turned away quickly, mumbling something about more bacon. She remembers! He thought, Oh Christ!

Dave woke up just as angry as when he'd gotten into bed. He threw the covers off and stormed into the bathroom. How could Emma let Steve stay the night? Is she seeing him? Images of Steve and Emma together formed in his mind. "Slut!" He said to himself.

He looked at himself in the bathroom mirror. Now hang on a minute if Emma is seeing Steve then Jackie must know about it. She is round Emma's house all the time after all. Why hasn't Jackie mentioned it to me? Jackie wouldn't let me go on making a fool of myself round Emma if she knew. So if Jackie hasn't said anything to me then there can't be anything going on, can there? I'll ask Jackie at work today. At least then I'll know where I stand.

It was about ten in the morning when he'd driven past Emma's house. The curtains were drawn in the living room but the Detective's car was still outside the house. He'd thought that killing the Detective's ex-wife would be enough of a message to make him steer clear of Emma's house but instead it had seemed to bring them closer.

He had to make her leave the house. While she was in there he couldn't get at her. It had become harder to watch her knowing that the police had placed surveillance outside. It was so much easier to keep tabs on her when she was working at the bar. Why wouldn't she go back to work? She couldn't stay at home forever with the police watching her. Life had to go on but patience wasn't a virtue he possessed, so how could he get her into a place where he could get her back for good. Maybe it was time to up the game.

Chapter Fourteen

Dave was down in the cellar changing a couple of kegs when Jackie rolled into work.

"Hi Dave, how are you today?" Jackie said as she grabbed some of the bottled drinks to take to the bar and fill up in the fridge.

"Hi Jackie, I'm not too bad but I have problem, well a question I need to ask you really." Dave said.

"Really?" Jackie said, already having an inkling of an idea of what Dave was going to ask. "Fire away."

"I'll be up in a minute," Dave replied, "I'll speak to you up stairs before we open."

"Ok." Jackie replied. He certainly wasn't himself today and Jackie was already starting to dread what the shift was going to be like. "When you come up can you bring me those bottles over there, then I won't have to come back down and you'll have my undivided attention."

"Sure."

Jackie went back up to the bar and started to load the bottles in the fridge.

Geoff finally showed his face shortly after eleven-thirty and busied himself with the very hard job of placing the ashtrays on the tables. Jackie knew he was the landlord but sometimes he could be so lazy. He often went out leaving Dave and her to run the pub but at least he was happier now. They had yet to meet his new 'friend' Rose because she had a baby and she didn't believe in bringing babies into a bar.

"Hi." Dave said, waking Jackie up from her thoughts as he placed the bottles down on the floor beside her. He looked like he hadn't slept too well, as if he had the weight of the world on his shoulders.

"So what's up hun?" Jackie asked, standing up and leaning against the bar as Dave began to spill out what was currently going on in his brain.

Geoff placed the last ashtray on the final table and turned to walk towards the bar. Jackie was leaning against the bar talking with Dave like they didn't have any more work to do before the pub opened. He just got in earshot when he heard Emma's name and stopped dead in his tracks.

"Well, I went round there last night and Steve was asleep on the chair, she was asleep on the sofa and two bottles of whisky were empty on the table." Dave said, "Are you sure she isn't seeing him?"

"Look Dave, I asked her over breakfast this morning and Emma assured me that there is nothing going on. You've got nothing to be worried about, she isn't ready for a relationship yet so you're still in with a chance."

"A chance? So she does have feelings for him then?" Dave said.

"To be honest, as far as I can make out, Emma likes him as much as she likes you and that's purely on a friendship basis, nothing more. With what she's been through recently surely you can understand that. You just need to be patient and then something may present itself." Jackie said turning back to her bottles. She had her suspicions that something more was going on between Steve and Emma but she wasn't going to tell Dave until she had concrete proof. He'd be gutted.

Dave's first steady girlfriend had walked out on him and since then he'd become so insecure. His jealousy had ruined the last three relationships he'd had and it seemed that it was going to end this one before it even had a chance to start. No, she definitely couldn't let him know that she thought Emma was already seeing Steve.

"Besides," Jackie said, deciding it was time to end this conversation before she got herself into trouble so deep she'd never be able to talk her way out of it. "You've known her longer than Steve, that's got to count for something. Your friendship has got to be stronger and true love always starts with friendship. I think she'll pick you over him any day."

"Thanks Jackie." Dave said, the green-eyed monster subdued for the time being.

So, Emma is seeing Steve, Geoff thought, All along I thought Emma was in love with Dave but she was leading him on, just like she'd done to me. Geoff turned and headed into the kitchen. He'd heard enough.

Steve sat at his mother's house waiting for her to finish cooking and call him through for lunch. The boys were upstairs in their room playing war with their Action Men that he had collected for them from Mary's place before coming back via the office. While he was waiting, Steve had decided to read the Psychologists Profile Report that he had 'fallen' into the bag containing some items from his office, unbeknownst to Bill who was busy talking through the case with Nick Fisher down the hallway.

Psychological Profile – Rosehill Rapist.

It's a man aged between twenty-five and thirty-five. Physically strong and well proportioned in build with a possible interested in bodybuilding or martial arts.

His mother left him with his father when he was young and he despised her for leaving him because his father abused him. He was teased at school and found it difficult to get on with the other children, playing truant for most of his lessons.

He hasn't had many relationships with women and ones he has had have ended after a short period of time. He will have had one solid relationship where he was deeply in love or even possibly married and this could be the trigger to his behaviour. My opinion is that this relationship was very violent due to jealousy and this has left him with pent up anger towards her in particular but could also be towards other woman making it hard to move if they have split.

He is insecure, very jealous by nature and feels the need to dominate women. He fantasizes about bondage and rape and indulges these fantasies of sex and violence with magazines and videos.

He is a loner with possibly a couple of male 'drinking buddies' but he has no close friends, as he likes to keep himself to himself. He is either unemployed or works part-time in a job where he can watch women.

He likes to sum up his victims and chooses them because they look very like the woman he had his strongest relationship with. When he rapes and kills

them he feels he as though he is taking control over
her, possessing her. Something if she has left him, he
can no longer do.

"Dinner's ready!" Steve's mum called.

Chapter Fifteen

Time had passed quickly since Emma's rape. Christmas had been and gone nearly without incident, and the New Year had begun in earnest but the police still hadn't caught him. The phone calls had gone from one a day to one a week and even then the 'weekly call' wouldn't be made a week on the dot from the last one. It made it harder for Emma when the phone eventually rang because by then she would just be thinking, he's forgotten this week so maybe he's finally given up. It was like he knew her thoughts because as soon as she started thinking this the phone would ring. Emma was glad it wasn't as bad as it was at the start but she still couldn't totally relax and now she had another problem playing on her mind. Dave or Steve or no love life, what to do? Emma didn't know. Maybe she should stick to no love life although she did feel kind of jealous of Jackie and Tony. It would be nice to have someone to talk to and hug occasionally.

Dave was such a lovely man. He made her laugh with his silly jokes, he was very good looking and Emma knew that Dave wanted to be with her. He'd popped over Christmas morning to see how she was doing. In fact, now she was thinking about it, Dave had popped by at least once, maybe even twice a week, every week since he'd found out what had happened to her even though she'd clearly stated that she wasn't ready for a relationship. You couldn't say that he wasn't determined.

Steve, like Dave, was very good looking but he was a little more serious and despite what had happened while they were drunk the night of his ex-wife's murder, Emma still couldn't be sure that Steve definitely wanted to be with her. He had hardly spoken to her since the day after their kiss and drunken embrace. He still popped by and called at the scheduled times but he was always very distant when they spoke. Emma couldn't read Steve like she could Dave. Did Steve believe that it just a moment of drunken temptation and nothing more? Emma was sure that there had been something more that night. When he had kissed her before they'd started drinking it had felt really good, there was definitely something there then. Had Steve remembered what they had nearly got up to and was too embarrassed to discuss it with her? Emma had been embarrassed the next day but now she felt a longing to explore the strong feelings that she felt for him.

These feelings weren't there with Dave but with Dave, she could be sure of a strong relationship because they were good friends. However, even Dave seemed strange at the moment, like he was checking up on her or maybe Emma was just being paranoid with everything going round in her head like washing tumbling around the drum of the washing machine. Anyway the more that Emma thought about it the more confused she became.

At least Emma had work to keep her mind off her problems for some of the time. She'd started back at Geoffrey's Bar just before Christmas and before she went back she'd made a point of taking Geoff to one side straight away and telling about what really happened and that the police were still keeping an eye on her because they hadn't caught him yet. As she told him Emma couldn't help but let a few tears out. It was still hard to talk about, especially when you were talking about it with someone who didn't already know what had happened.

"You should have told me Emma." Geoff said putting his large hands on her shoulders and pulling her into a bear hug. While hugging her Geoff began rubbing her back and he told her that he wasn't happy that she had lied to him but did say if she needed anymore time off, it wouldn't be problem. Emma tried to pull away from this uncomfortable invasion of space but couldn't.

"And if you need anything, anything at all." Geoff whispered in her ear. "You come and see me."

Emma pulled away quickly as Geoff's grip loosened and he started to stroke her hair. An uncomfortable shiver ran down her spine and knowing that she needed this job to pay her bills, Emma changed the subject by saying that if she had any more time off she would go completely mad with boredom.

Emma was relieved that Geoff didn't mention the incident that had happened between them before her rape but she knew that it wasn't far from the front of his mind. It this new creepy incident came as a shock to her since Jackie had told her he was always off visiting his new girlfriend Rose. Anyway, Emma decided to avoid him as much as possible, she had enough problems to contend with, she didn't need to add Geoff to her list. However, she was beginning to get more and more uncomfortable with the way he watched her while she was working behind the bar. Every time she looked round he seemed to be there, just staring at her with piggish pale blue eyes. Then, when he realized that she'd caught him staring, he'd give her a grin and a wink and then disappear from the bar for a while. Emma just kept reminding herself that she'd only gone back to work there because bills needed to be paid and it was easier to explain to Geoff why she had quit than explaining to a new employer why she had been out of work for so long. At least while she was earning Emma could keep her eyes open for something else.

Emma had wanted to talk to Jackie about all this but she was out a lot more these days. Her relationship with Tony seemed to be steaming along and Jackie didn't seem to have a lot of time left for anything or anyone else despite the fact that Jackie had moved into Emma's house on New Year's Eve. Jackie had told her landlord where he could stuff his rent and moved all her belongings into Emma's after his failure to fix the bad electrics in her flat. It was good because it worked out much cheaper for the both of them than living in separate places and helped Emma with the bills for her place and now that Jackie was living with Emma it meant that Emma needed to meet Tony. So today Tony was picking Jackie up and meeting Emma for the first time.

Jackie was upstairs getting ready when the doorbell rang. Emma got up from the kitchen table where she and Dave sat enjoying a cup of coffee and a chat about work, and went to answer the door.

"Hello," she said, "You must be Tony, I'm Emma, come on in. Jackie's upstairs busy getting ready, she shouldn't be long. Would you like a drink while you're waiting?"

"Yes, a coffee would be nice. We can't stop long though I've booked a table for dinner." Tony said. His voice was deep and his reply was brusque.

"Come through to the kitchen and I'll make you one." Emma said smiling, ignoring his abruptness and putting it down to nerves. "How do you like it?"

"Black, no sugar."

Emma took him through to the kitchen, introducing Tony to Dave, who had also popped round to meet Jackie's amazing man, as she filled the kettle. Emma took a good look at him while the kettle boiled. Tony was very tall, about six foot five maybe more. He seemed quite broad shouldered but that didn't balance out the profound height he seemed to possess. He wore baggy Chino-styled trousers, a white T-shirt and leather jacket with the collar stuck up. He also wore a pair of dark Rayban sunglasses and had a slight growth of beard, which was all the rage at the moment. His hair was dark and slicked back with a lot of gel which made it very shiny. Personally, Emma couldn't see what Jackie saw in him. He looked like a reject from a Miami Vice audition.

Emma poured his cup of coffee and handed it to him. As the cups passed hands she couldn't help but notice his extremely large hands.

"Do you mind if I have a cigarette?" He asked.

"No, go ahead." Emma said.

Tony offered them around and Dave joined him in one and used the opportunity to ask Tony what sort of music he liked.

Just as the conversation was starting to get somewhere, Jackie came bounding down the stairs. She greeted Tony by standing on her tip-toes to give him a peck on the cheek and said, "Hello lover."

Tony finished his cigarette and then quickly drank his coffee down in one large gulp. "Is it all right if I use your toilet before we go?" He asked Emma, his voice sounding more relaxed than when he'd first got there.

"Sure," Emma said, "It's upstairs, first on the right."

As soon as Tony left the room, Emma turned to Jackie. "He seems nice enough, very tall though." Emma knew she'd lied but she couldn't tell Jackie the truth. Tony gave her the creeps but if Jackie liked him then so be it. She wasn't going to grumble so long as her friend was happy. Mind you if she thought about it, most men gave her the creeps nowadays, except for Dave and Steve.

Jackie was laughing, "You know what?" She said, "I must look just like what a bungalow would look next to the Empire State Building. Little and Large are nothing compared to us." She carried on giggling.

After about ten minutes Dave said, "He's taking a long time up there!"

"Maybe he's fallen in!" Emma said.

"Tony always takes a long time in the toilet." Jackie said. "He did when I first met him."

"Maybe he's got a thing about toilets!" Dave said, cracking up.

Tony came back into the room while they were all still laughing. "We'd better go." He said, in a 'we are not amused' tone.

"Shall we take my car?" Jackie said.

"I was hoping you'd say that. Mine's in the garage for a service." Tony said.

"I'll probably be back late, so don't wait up." Jackie said, winking at Emma.

"Okay," Emma said, "I'll see you later. Have a good time." And she winked back.

Emma walked them to the door, watching them get into Jackie's car and as started the engine the music blared out like a disco from the cassette player. Jackie turned and waved at Emma. Emma waved back. As they pulled away from the curb, Tony turned to look back at Emma, removed his sunglasses and grinning from ear to ear like a Cheshire cat, he waved a sarcastically exaggerated wave at her. His ice-cold blue eyes were staring straight at her. Teasing her. Taunting her. Laughing at her. Knowing that she couldn't believe her eyes. Emma felt like she was going to faint.

"Oh my god!" She screamed when she finally found her voice. "Oh my god, it's him!"

"What's up?" Dave called as he came running from the kitchen.

"It's him!" Emma screamed. "It's the man who raped me!"

"Where?" Dave asked as he stood at her side frantically looking around to try and see him. Poised, ready to run at him and beat the living daylights out of him.

"In the car with Jackie. Jackie's boyfriend Tony is the man who raped me!"

Chapter Sixteen

Detective Harris pulled up about half an hour after Emma had convinced Dave that she wasn't going mad and seeing things. Dave had already called Detective Fisher and the doctor, who was administering Emma with a light sedative to calm her down but Emma wanted Steve. Dave didn't like the fact that she wanted him. Detective Fisher was in charge of the case now.

Emma had been hysterical since Jackie had left and kept saying things like, "I knew there was something wrong about him. Why didn't I say something? Why didn't I stop her?" Dave could understand what Emma was going through but she wasn't the one at fault. He had tried to convince her that she couldn't have known but still she carried on like she could have stopped this from happening. Dave explained this to Steve as they sat in the kitchen waiting for the doctor and Nick Fisher to leave. It wasn't a pleasant atmosphere to be in after the initial fill-in had happened. Both these men, longing to be the man that Emma would choose if and when she finally decided to go back to dating again, clearly not wanting to be in the same room together let alone be civil to each other and here they were having to make small talk as they both wished the other one would leave.

This atmosphere didn't change as they left the kitchen to move into the sitting room after the doctor had gone. Dave quickly sat down on the sofa with his arm round Emma comforting her as if to claim his territory. Steve, who briefly stopped in the hall to chat to Nick Fisher as he left, sat in the armchair by the window. Steve jealously wished it were him sitting over there. He knew that Dave cared a lot about Emma but Steve believed that he could love her more. "Are you sure it was him Emma?" Steve asked.

"I'm positive." Emma said a little calmer now that the drug had taken effect. "It was definitely him. He was leering at me out of the car window, and loving every minute of it." Dave tightened his hold around Emma as she took in a deep breath to stay calm, reassuring her that he was there to protect her. "Just to prove the point, he even waved at me as Jackie drove off."

I talked to the men on watch on my way in and none of them got a very good look at him because he had the collar of his jacket pulled up and those sunglasses on. You had informed them that Jackie's boyfriend, Tony was coming round so, just like you, they were expecting him as friend and weren't really paying much attention until you started shouting and by then it was too late. He'd obviously planned this all along and I wouldn't be surprised if Jackie hadn't told him about the men on watch outside. Anyway, I've spoken to Nick Fisher and he's got policemen driving round Ipswich looking for the car. I'm afraid that all we can do now is wait patiently until they find it. Jackie obviously doesn't know it's him, so she'll be safe." Steve said, trying to make things look a lot better than they actually were. He wondered whether Emma believed him.

"Shall I go and make us a strong cup of coffee each? I think we need it." Dave said changing the subject, getting up from the sofa and heading off to the kitchen.

"The mug!" Emma blurted out, making both men jump and look at her as if she had finally gone round the bend.

"What!" They both said together.

"The mug that Tony had his coffee in, couldn't we get some

prints off it?" Emma asked.

"Where is it?" Steve asked.

"It's in the kitchen." Emma said frantically.

Dave face dropped and he said, "There's only one problem."

"What?" Emma and Steve said simultaneously.

"I washed it up while you were at the door seeing them off."

"Then I guess you're right Steve, there is nothing else we can do except wait." And, with tears welling up in her eyes, Emma got up and left the room.

"Will she be all right?" Steve asked, concerned. He cared a lot about her but he could see that it was hopeless she wasn't ready for a relationship.

"I think so." Dave said, thinking it would be better that she was left alone to have a good cry. "Would you still like that cup of coffee?" Dave asked politely, secretly wishing he'd just bugger off so he could look after Emma on his own.

"Yes, that would be nice." Steve replied thinking I am going to stay for a bit whether you want me here or not.

Suddenly there came a scream from upstairs. Steve and

Dave both bolted up the stairs and into Emma's bedroom with Dave winning the race but only because Steve was sat down. They found Emma rooted to the spot. She looked as white as a sheet. On the bed was a photo of Jackie with a bunch of white roses in her arms, and beside the picture was a white rosebud, splattered with something that resembled blood.

"It's a picture from their first date," Emma mumbled, "taken while I was in hospital recovering. He's known what he's been doing right from the start....." She trailed off at that point and started to weep.

Dave grabbed Emma and took her downstairs while Steve picked up the photo and the rose with his handkerchief and took them downstairs to the police car outside.

"Run forensics on this Peter and check the photo for prints." Steve said. "Let's see if these can tell us anything about this sly bastard. If you hear any news on Jackie, give me a call to let me know what's going on and don't tell anyone that you're doing so. I think I am going to stay here for a while." And with that he went back inside. There wasn't much else he could do, except wait. Steve wished that this would lead to an arrest, for Emma's sake and Mary's. He couldn't wait to see the killer behind bars but at the moment things just seemed to be getting more and more complicated. I mean, who would have thought that Jackie was dating the killer all along. It's no wonder he always seemed one step ahead. When Steve came back in the sedative had taken effect and Emma was curled up on the sofa under a blanket, so he went and sat with Dave in the kitchen until she woke up.

Steve stayed with them both, even when Nick Fisher came back with some mug shots and a police artist he sat himself out of the way but stayed in ear shot.

It started out fine with the artist but as the drawing went on Emma and Dave couldn't decide on which chin Tony had or even what shape his nose was. It nearly caused an argument and despite how Steve felt, he didn't want to be involved in an argument about noses and chins so stayed where he was. He heard Nick he felt it best to go with Emma's decision because she was the victim and had seen more of his face after all, so her description was bound to be the better one. Once again Nick left but Steve decided to stay on and he could tell that Dave was getting more than a little annoyed at his presence, which made him want to stay more.

It was five o'clock, three hours since Jackie had driven off with Tony in her car and they still hadn't heard anything. It was like they had vanished into thin air. There were the three of them, all sat round the table with their plates of food in front of them. Homemade Spaghetti Bolognese with garlic bread. Emma sat there pushing her food around the plate, not even attempting to eat it. It made her wonder why she'd bothered to even cook it. At least she wasn't the alone; Dave wasn't doing much better with his. Just picking at his food, seemingly not caring if it slide off the fork or not and then giving up altogether. Dave pushed his plate to one side looking at Emma apologetically. The only one who had a clean plate was Steve. He turned to Dave and said, "If you don't want yours, can I have it?"

"Go ahead." Dave said and pushed his plate towards Steve.

Steve looked at Emma, who was staring at him. "You're a brilliant cook." He said, thinking if only she was cooking just for him. "I haven't had grub like this since...." He stopped talking and drifted off....Since before he'd left his wife. His wife, who was now dead because of that bastard who had now got Jackie and he couldn't do a thing about it because he'd been taken off the case. The killer was probably in the process of doing the same to Jackie as he'd done to Mary while they were sat here eating. Well, he *was* eating. All of a sudden Steve's appetite seemed to have disappeared. Come hell or high water he had to get back on this case.

"Since when?" Emma prompted bringing him back from his thoughts.

"Since I was married." He answered looking down at his plate, so that they couldn't see what he was thinking.

"You were married? You don't look the type. A bit of a cliché there, aren't you!" Dave piped up snidely and killing what little conversation there was.

Silence once again shrouded the table, until Steve's police radio broke it.

"Excuse me." He said, leaving the table and walking into the hall to receive the message.

"Well that was nice of you Dave!" Emma berated. "Tony killed his ex-wife and now his kids are motherless."

"How the hell was I supposed to know?" Dave said. "I'm not psychic!"

They both shut up quick as Steve came back in the room.

Emma looked at him hopefully, "Have they found them?" She asked.

"No, I'm afraid not." Steve said, "Pete just called to let me know the results of the lab test. The red stains on the rose have been identified human blood. As for fingerprints, there were none. I'm sorry."

Emma felt her eyes filling up with tears again. Pushing her plate aside, Emma got up and left the room, saying, "Why couldn't he just leave me alone?"

"I'd better go." Said Steve, not wanting to leave while Emma was like this but knowing that if he didn't he'd never get back on this case. Plus he couldn't bear to sit around watching Dave getting close to Emma when that was exactly what he wanted to do. He pulled on his coat. "I'll speak to Nick about organizing some other means of watch on the house, possibly getting a man in house instead and I'll get someone round to change the locks. He'll probably have Jackie's key. Would you let Emma know that Detective Fisher is going to be checking through Jackie's belongings to see whether she has a telephone number or address or maybe something in a diary to say where they met up previously? Anything like that could help."

"Okay." Dave said and walked him to the door. After letting Steve out and he decided to see how Emma was. She was going to need his support more than ever now. Dave went upstairs, knocked and then opened the door to her bedroom without waiting to be invited in. Emma was sitting on the bed with her knees drawn up close to her chest, rocking back and forth. He walked over and sat on the edge of the bed.

"What am I going to do Dave?" Emma asked, looking him straight in the eyes. "Since this has happened I've got you, Jackie and Steve involved. Steve's wife was murdered by Tony and now Jackie's with him somewhere, probably dead already. You're probably next on his list. It seems that it's a priority to him kill anyone who's come into contact with me. I'm endangering everybody's lives. What am I going to do?"

Dave pulled her close to him and held her as tight as he could. "He isn't going to get me, don't you worry. I haven't been doing bodybuilding for all these years to let some killer get the better of me." He said and kissed her reassuringly on the forehead. "Look, I know you said you want to take things slow but remember I'm always going to be here for you and if that means protecting you as well then I will do. I can take care of myself but most importantly I'll take care of you too, even if it is just as a friend." Dave pulled Emma into him, inhaling the scent of her hair as he stroked it and wishing that he could be more than friends but knowing it would be a long road before any changes in their relationship happened.

As Dave held her close, stroking her hair, Emma closed her

eyes and all of a sudden it wasn't Dave who was holding her, it was Steve. She sighed.

Steve drove back to the station to catch up on his paperwork, and speak to Nick about organising a new watch on the house. Steve wished he could do more for Emma. He wished it were him who was comforting her now, holding her in his arms, and not Dave. It was a good job his skin didn't change colour to match his moods, because at the moment it would be a very jealous looking green.

Lying on the sofa bed, Dave watched the daylight appear through the crack in the curtains. He hadn't slept a wink all night. Emma had if you could call it sleeping. He'd gone to look in on her several times to see how she was doing. She was tossing and turning. Dave wished that he could get into her nightmare and tell her everything was going to be all right. Kill off all the baddies and make her dream a pleasant one but Dave knew that he could never get into her dreams as much as he knew that everything wasn't going to be all right. The truth was Jackie was probably dead already and nothing he could do was going to make *that* all right.

Dave went back down stairs and lit a cigarette. Just then the telephone rang, waking him up from his thoughts. He picked it up. "Hello," He said, "Who is it?"

"Dave, it's Steve. They've found Jackie's car..."

Emma, who had come down to get a drink, entered the living room. "Who is it?" She asked, sleepily.

"It's Steve," Dave said, "They've found Jackie's car."

"Let me speak to him!" Emma said urgently.

He handed her the receiver. "Hello Steve. Is Jackie ok?"

"I'm sorry Emma we've only found the car." Steve said, wishing he could have something more positive to tell her.

"That's means he's still got her." Emma said slowly, pausing for thought. "Or he's killed her."

"No, I don't think he's done that. The car was completely burnt out though. That means no fingerprints. I think he's taken her somewhere. There were a second set tyre tracks from where the car was left and drag marks to where the other vehicle was left. I reckon he's taken her some place where he can hide her without anybody noticing. I'd also put a bet on where we found the car is miles away from where he's keeping her. I'm not going to get your hopes up though. I'm afraid to say we've got a very clever man here and it might be very hard to find him. I just hope that we get to him in time to save Jackie's life. I just know he won't kill her yet. My gut feeling is she's worth more to him while she's alive. Is everything all right there?" He asked.

"Yes the cats still smiling." And with that they both hung up.

Chapter Seventeen

Jackie came round to find herself in a gloomy room with only two candles to keep it from plunging into total darkness. She tried to look at her watch but found that she was tied to the chair she was sitting on. Jackie looked around the room and noticed an alarm clock by the boarded up window. Illuminated by one of the candles, she could see it said five-forty. The last thing that she remembered was going back to the multi-story car park after the meal with Tony. This was about three-thirty. Tony! Where was Tony? He'd said that he'd be right behind her but he had to go to the little boy's room before they went back to his place. Jackie was just walking back to the car and fumbling in her handbag for her keys when something hit her on the back of the head. The next thing she knew was that she'd woken up here. Wherever here was?

Jackie started to call for help. After a while she decided it was useless, it was obvious that no one could hear her, and gave up.

Jackie tried to wrestle with the ropes that bound her wrists together. They were done up so tight that she could feel her wrists getting sore every time she tried moving. Jackie soon gave up on this also, realizing that without being able to look she couldn't see if she was making it better or worse.

Jackie had a good look at her surroundings. If she ever got free she would probably need a quick means of escape. There was a front door but, looking at the arched glass panel at the top, Jackie could clearly see that it was boarded up just like the windows.

It was an average sized room with no carpet, only floorboards. These were covered in a thick layer of dust. In the dim light you could just make out some footprints in the dust where someone had walked and a reasonable sized streak from the door to where she sat. Jackie presumed that the streak was from when her kidnapper had dragged her along the floor to the chair that she was now tied to.

The wallpaper, which was really old and yellowed, was peeling off the walls like the skin of a leper revealing the crumbling plaster. Some of this plaster had chunks missing from it.

Jackie tried not to move her head round too quickly realising when she did that she had a terrible headache that must have come from the blow to the back of her head earlier.

The place was very cold and had a terrible stench, which Jackie seemed to recognize but couldn't place. It was like a damp smell mingled with the disgusting odour you get in men's toilets and then there was another smell that she couldn't place. As Jackie sat there thinking about it, she suddenly remembered the time she'd found a dead rat in the cellar of her old ground floor flat. Its body had started to decay and it was covered in maggots. That was the smell. She felt like she wanted to be sick.

From where Jackie was sitting she could see that the kitchen window was also boarded up. It must be a derelict house, she thought. Her quick conclusion then led to another more dreadful one. No one would ever know she was here.

Jackie must have dozed off for a while because she found

herself waking up to movement in the house. It was coming from the kitchen which she now couldn't see into because the door had been shut. She looked over at the clock. Ten past eight.

"Who's there?" She shouted nervously.

She paused for a minute and then, when no one answered, she said, "Why are you keeping me here?"

No answer. She then said bravely, "I know that you're in there, I can here you moving around."

The door opened and a man in a balaclava stood in the doorway. It's you!" Jackie said, shocked to see him standing there. "You're the man who raped my friend Emma! What do you want with me?"

He didn't answer.

"Where's Tony?" Jackie asked, getting frustrated at not receiving any answers.

"Tony's safe, believe me." He said smiling.

"What have you done with him?" You haven't killed him, have you?"

The man began pulling off his balaclava.

Jackie couldn't believe her eyes as the balaclava was pulled away to reveal Tony's face.

"Surprise, surprise, the unexpected hits you between the eyes." He smiled laughing at his witty impersonation of Cilla Black singing the opening song to her programme on television. Still laughing he said, "I told you he was safe!"

"You! You're the one who raped Emma."

"Yes, I'm the one." He said proudly.

"How could you? And then take me out on dates as though nothing had happened." Jackie said not believing that this was really happening to her.

Jackie's mind rolled back to one of the first conversations she'd had with Emma when they'd arrived back from the hospital. Emma had been staring out the window when Jackie had come downstairs from having a bath. "Are you ok?" Jackie had asked as she walked up behind her.

"I was just looking at all the people walking by the house." Emma said vacantly as she stared out the window. "Look," She said. "Do you see that man over there?"

"Yes?" Jackie had replied, puzzled, wondering where Emma

was going to go next with the conversation.

"It could be him."

"What?"

"He could be the man who raped me." Emma said and then looked further down the road and pointed at another man. "Or it could be him." A car passed by the window and Emma pointed again. "Or him."

"Emma..." Jackie started.

"Don't you see Jackie any of the men that pass by my house could be the man who raped me. He said he's watching me which means it could be anyone." A tear slowly ran down the side of her cheek. "Promise me you'll take your car wherever you go?"

"Emma..."

"Promise me?" Emma interrupted.

"I promise." Jackie had said and hugged her as if to seal the deal.

Jackie couldn't believe what was happening. It had been one of the 'any men' that Emma had spoken to her about. And not just any man, it was Tony. Jackie looked up at him and softly asked, "Are you going to kill me?"

"No. Not yet anyway." He said grinning at the thought. "But you'll get what you deserve in good time, just like Emma will."

There was a moment of silence as Jackie wished to God that this was a dream and she would wake up any minute in her bed at Emma's house. Then she asked, "Why are you doing this?"

"Emma's got to be punished. She's got to realize that it doesn't matter where she runs or what she does to try and hide from me I will always find her. Emma will always belong to me."

"But Emma doesn't belong to you what makes you think that she does?" Jackie asked not knowing where her bravery was coming from. Here she was arguing with a man who could turn around and kill her at anytime. She must be mad but she needed to know.

"Look, I wanted Emma and I took her and now she belongs to me. At the moment she's being a bad girl. She should never have left me and changed her name. She shouldn't be acting like a slut with the barman and the detective. She's mine and if I can't have her, I'm going to make sure that no one can. I'm going to give her one more chance to love me like she did in the beginning. Emma should love only me, she's mine and that's the only way it can be."

"What are you talking about? What beginning? Emma had never met you until you raped her, let alone loved you! She's never wanted you, never liked you, and certainly never loved you! She hates you!"

"Liar! Emma loves me, I know she does. She's always loved me." Tony shouted getting frustrated with the way the conversation was going.

"She doesn't love you. Just look at what you've did to her." Jackie challenged. "She doesn't love you, she hates you!"

"Shut up bitch!" He shouted, anger burning through his icy glare and his face turning red.

"Why should I? Don't you like the truth?"

"Shut up!" He yelled, slapping her round the face. "Shut up now or I'll cut your bloody tongue out!"

Jackie looked up at him; her face was burning down one side where it had come into contact with his hand. She couldn't believe that the wonderful man that she'd gotten to know over the past couple of months could be the same man who had raped her friend. The man whom she had fallen in love with in that short space of time, who she thought was the perfect gentleman and had spent the last couple of months dreaming of him asking her to marry him. How could Tony be a serial killer and rapist? Jackie just couldn't believe it, here was that man, the man she'd dreamed about spending the rest of her life with, threatening to cut her tongue out. Jackie couldn't believe it but, now in this room, looking at his face, she could see that he wasn't bluffing.

It was a few hours before Jackie spoke again and even then it was only to ask to go to the toilet. Tony released her hands from the chair. It was then that Jackie noticed he'd tied her hands together first and then tied them to the chair with a separate piece of rope. He followed holding on to the rope bound her wrists together as he pushed her up stairs to the bathroom. On the way up she noticed that the only ground floor exit that wasn't boarded up was the back door in the kitchen. Jackie tried to make a break for it but all she could do was struggle, his grip on her was like an iron vice.

There were no carpets upstairs either. The floors were just as dusty as those downstairs, and they had spots randomly dotted on them. It looked just like blobs of crimson paint. Jackie could tell by the state the house was in that it hadn't been lived in for years.

As Jackie entered the bathroom she noticed that the sink was stained with a rusty coloured substance. The thicker it got the more crimson it became. Probably the same paint she had seen on the floorboards on the landing. Who, in their right mind would pour this much paint in the sink and not wash it out?

As Jackie sat down on the toilet she got her question answered. In the bath was the same crimson liquid. She got back up, shoved back the grubby shower curtain and screamed. Hanging there, attached by several metal spikes to a makeshift wooden cross that had been firmly fixed to the ceiling was a girl of about sixteen. The spikes were hollowed out and sloped slightly downwards. Blood dripped from the ends. He'd also slashed her wrists and ankles and Jackie knew that from the way the blood was still dripping out that the girl hadn't been there long.

All the blood had collected in the bottom of the bath. It was about half way up the side of the bath. One body couldn't bleed that much, could it? Jackie wondered how many bodies it had taken already to get the half full bath. She started to feel dizzy as she looked and realized what the future held in store for her.

"Hurry up in there!" Tony shouted, making Jackie jump.

Jackie couldn't believe that this man could be what he was. Anybody walking down the street would say he was all right. He looked so normal but then, what was normal? Did she know what a murderer looked like? She'd seen pictures of Charles Manson he didn't look normal but what about the Yorkshire Ripper, the Boston Strangler or Ian Brady? They all looked normal. So, how could you tell apart the murderers from the normal people of this world if they all looked alike? Jackie wished she'd never met this man. Here he was holding her prisoner and Jackie knew that he was going to kill her soon. How could she get herself into this predicament? Was she ever going to get out of this alive?

Chapter Eighteen

"Tony! Tony!"

Tony knew that sound. It was his mother's voice screaming to him for help. And there he was, as regular as clockwork, back at his home in Jubilee Avenue, Stowmarket.

He looked to the top of the stairs where he saw a little five-year-old boy creeping to the edge of the banister and peering through the mahogany stained bars. With his white, blonde hair, he looked just like an angel in flannel-checked pyjamas. He knew that the little boys 'angelic' face was just a disguise for the monster that was about to start growing inside. For this 'angel's' name was Tony and, as he looked on, he saw the boy quietly watching the commotion that was unfolding downstairs. His expression, slightly scared to begin with, changed, as his mother's screams grew louder, calling for him, and a grin of pure evil began to develop on his innocent face. Turning the 'angelic' face into that of a child possessed.

Tony knew he was dreaming but the dream was more like a video playing over in his mind while he was sleeping. He knew twenty years ago, that night had happened for real. It was the night his father had gone too far. The night that his mother had finally learnt her lesson and, had from then on, started residing at the bottom of the garden along with Billy the goldfish, Harry the hamster, and Lady the dog with her still-born puppies.

Tony could remember that night so well. His mother and father were in a full-blown argument when he awoke. His mother had been screaming his name. Tony didn't know what the argument was about but he did know that his father always had to have things done the way he wanted them. His father always knew how to make sure that his authority was known and carried out as instructed.

He'll never forget the sound of his father swinging the poker through the air. It was so fast, whooshing and whistling through the air. The whistle, never tuneful, more like a high-pitched scream of a firework and always cut short by a dull thud followed by a scream of true pain from his mother's lips. Eventually, rasps of breath replaced the screams and finally followed by silence. Tony's father slowly calmed down and realized what he'd done. That was a big turning point for both Tony and his father.

Tony's father went around telling friends and family that Tony's mother had left them. They believed him of course. They had known how chauvinistic and oppressive he was and didn't think to question once what Tony's father was telling them. It wasn't the first argument they'd had. He beat her about at least once a month, especially when he was drunk. Everyone expected her to leave him eventually. They just assumed that she'd finally come to her senses. So they believed the lies he told them. Believed him that was, until the weekend at grandma's house.

His father had dropped him off outside the house, watching him walk to the door with his toy plane in one hand and his rucksack on his shoulder. As his Gran opened the door, his father drove away. They never had been very friendly. When they used to go to tea around there, his father usually stayed at home and Tony's mother made excuses for him by saying that he was working or something. He'd drop them off and then pick them up later, usually with smell of alcohol and cigarettes clinging to him like an invisible fog.

Anyway, it was Sunday teatime when the truth slipped out. What did his father expect anyway, Tony was only five going on six and believed everything that his father told him. They were all sat around the table eating cold meat sandwiches and cake, Tony, his grandma, his grandfather and his aunt who still lived at home. His aunt suggested that they should get the family album out after they'd finished eating. "I bet Tony would love to see some pictures of his mum when she was a little girl." She'd said, smiling.

"I wish we knew where she'd gone." His grandfather had said, "It's not like our Rosemary. She would always write to us to let us know where she was."

"Daddy say's that there aren't any post-boxes in heaven." Tony blurted out.

All the faces at the dinner table turned to face Tony. The looks of disbelieve on their faces mirroring each other.

"What did you say?" His grandfather had asked.

Tony repeated what he'd said and then added, "But don't worry granddad, she's looking after Billy, Harry and Lady. Isn't mummy good?"

Tony's Grandmother hurriedly left the room quickly followed by his aunt. His grandfather reached into his pocket and pulled out some change and left the house for the telephone box at the end of the street.

When Tony's father came to pick him up from his Grandparents there was a police car sat out front waiting for him. Tony never saw his father again.

If only his father could see him now, He'd be so proud.

Tony tapped his logbook that sat next to him on his bedside table; it was always a good read when he was feeling low. Sometimes it gave him a hard on just to read what he'd done to the women he'd murdered. Occasionally it made him go out and murder someone else, so he could try and relive it but each one was different. Sometimes it would be more exciting than the last one and sometimes it would leave him disappointed and angry.

Tony had finished last night's entry before he'd fallen asleep. He'd written about the wonderful evening he'd spent with Jackie.

Oh, how she'd screamed. Tony liked it better when they screamed. Although Jackie wasn't really his type, he'd still had a strong orgasm. He had a good imagination; which was lucky really he'd imagined that Jackie was Emma. Maybe one day he'd manage to get past the security outside Emma's house and bring her back here, then he would no longer have to imagine.

Once he'd got her back he would make her change her name back to Rose. He hated calling her Emma. Why did she have to change her name anyway, Rose was a much nicer name. His mum was called Rose and if it was a good enough name for his mum it was a good enough name for her. Besides, changing her name would never disguise the fact that she was his Rose. She belonged to him and nothing would keep him away from her.

Jackie was limp when he'd sat her back on the chair. Tony did try to put her clothes on but she just flopped about like a dead fish. At that thought he'd checked her pulse. There was one. He'd have to be a bit more careful next time. He couldn't afford to kill her off just yet.

Tony's thoughts returned back to his childhood. After his

father left he went to live with grandmother and grandfather. He can remember his grandmother crying every time she looked at the photos of his mother. In the end his grandfather suggested that they take all the photos, place them in a box and put them in the attic. It seemed to be easier after that.

It was after Easter when Tony started his new school. From day one he didn't fit in. First it was because he was the new boy. When someone else new came along he knew it would stop. That someone else came along about two months later; it didn't stop though, the new boy just joined in with the teasing. As the years went on the teasing just grew worse. When Tony started high school he found the library a good place to hide at break times but they even found him there.

They teased him about his clothes and his basin hair cut. Living with grandparents didn't help matters. His grandfather would cut his hair so he wouldn't have to go to the barbers and spend money unnecessarily. When it came to clothes shopping he'd tried so hard to talk them into buying him clothes like all the other kids wore. He could still hear his grandfather saying, *"Those clothes won't last five minutes the way you run around at school. Always playing football and fighting with the other boys. Until you can look after your clothes you'll have to have what we can afford."*

And because they'd insist on clothes that were hard wearing, they lasted longer and that was probably the worst thing about them. Even growing out of them didn't help because they would just go out and buy him some more of the same. The irony was if they had just bought him the same clothes as the other kids wore then he wouldn't end up getting into the fights that ruined his clothes, as the fights he got into were mostly due to the clothes he wore.

The summer holidays came and went. The Christmas holidays came and went. He never wanted to go back to school at the end of them. Each time he told himself that the teasing wouldn't happen anymore but it did.

Anyway, he'd had the best of times while he'd been alone. He'd spent many a year just taking the teasing, and now at fourteen years old Tony decided that things were going to change. Just lately he'd been spending a lot of time in his secret place. He'd found it when being chased one day. It was through a fence at the end of the playing meadow and was obscured by brambles and other foliage.

It was also at this age that Tony started getting interested in his schoolwork, mainly Biology but also some Chemistry. He borrowed some books out of the library on Biology. He enjoyed the dissection parts best. Tony spent many hours teaching himself dissection and anatomy with the books, starting with a frog from the pond in the back yard, followed by his cousin's hamster and then came the black cat from up the road.

He'd kill them by suffocation; the frog and the hamster were easy, only having to apply a little pressure but the cat was a lot harder. It fought back more, scratching his arms and trying to bite him. Its will to live was amazing, even exciting. In the end Tony had used a piece of flex that he'd found in the shed, wrapping it round its neck and just pulling it tighter and tighter.

Tony had found that it was a lot more exciting killing the cat! It was a good job that his grandparents were out; it made enough noise to wake the dead. Anyway, after killing them he'd take them to school in his old lunch box. Tony told his grandmother that one of the bigger boys had stolen it at school before beating him up and that he couldn't remember which one it was. Then when lunchtime came round he'd take it to his secret place and practice. You would assume that most kids interested in dissection would go into a career as a doctor but Tony didn't want to save lives he wanted the power to take them. It felt good to be God.

He'd found a knife in his grandfather's attic. He'd only gone up to find a photo of his mother for a school project. It was a pretty knife, covered in patterns, and in the middle of the handle was a pretty sparkling stone that if you looked close enough, and were in the right light, sparkled with all the colours of the rainbow. He knew that his grandfather wouldn't miss it, so he'd slipped it into his sock and had gone back to his room, the photo of his mother and his school project forgotten for the time being.

After a lot of practice Tony became quite good, especially once he'd learnt how to keep the knife sharp. His secret place wasn't just for dissecting animals. Tony stole some of his grandfather's cigarettes and started smoking. Also he became interested in girls while in his secret place.

One day Tony had gone to his uncle's with his grandfather to drop off a birthday present. For once his uncle had been in. His uncle invited them both in for a coffee and with Tony needing to use the bathroom, his grandfather had agreed. After using the bathroom he'd passed his uncle's bedroom. Something from under the bed caught his eye. Tony could hear his grandfather and uncle talking and laughing, so he tiptoed in. As Tony got down on his hands and knees, he could see that they were magazines of nude women posing in different positions. As Tony stared at the covers he felt different and a strange thing happened inside his trousers. Liking this feeling, Tony wondered where he could hide a few. He crept downstairs and wrapped some up in his jacket. Tony made a mental note to bring a bag with him next time.

After a while dissecting animals was forgotten about and he spent most of his time reading dirty magazines and smoking. Tony started to compare the girls at school to the women in the magazine and began to wonder what the girls looked like without their clothes on. He wished he could find out.

After the Christmas holiday a new girl joined his class. Her name was Sandra. She had freckles and ginger pigtails that the boys constantly tugged on as they teased her. Sandra was a bit on the skinny side but she nearly had the biggest breasts in class except for 'Lucy big tits' that was as hers were the biggest. Anyway, for some unknown reason Sandra was the only girl in school who showed any interest in him, maybe because he didn't pull her pigtails like the other guys. She always used to put her bony arse on the chair next to his in almost all his classes and at dinnertime she'd taken to following him around, which at times was quite a pain. While she was following him around Tony couldn't sneak off to his secret place and look at his magazines. He'd walk around trying to get rid of her, by the time the bell rang at the end of school he was dying for a smoke.

Finally Tony decided that enough was enough and he

decided to sort out his little problem. Tony formulated a plan but he wasn't sure that it would work though. Mind you, if Sandra was that keen on him, maybe she'd do him a favour.

Tony decided it was time to show her his secret place. He'd hid his magazines up of course but then if he played his cards right, he might not need them today.

First break went just like clockwork. Sandra had followed him around the whole time like a sheep in short navy blue skirt and gingham blouse. She had white shoes, white tights, and had little blue gingham bows in her pigtails. Sandra didn't come close to the women in the magazines but she'd make do. Tony just had to see what a real girl looked and felt like.

At lunchtime Sandra had started to follow him around as usual. She had a big surprise when Tony walked over to her and said hello. It took him long enough to do it and he can remember just how much his heart was beating.

Sandra said, "Hi," and blushed from head to toe, then started giggling and looked at her feet.

"What you doing?" He'd asked.

"Just walking about." Sandra said red-faced and still looking at her feet. "What you doing?"

"Oh, just walking about." Tony replied. "Do you want to know a secret? You mustn't say anything to anyone. If you do I'll have to kill you."

"Yeah, I won't tell."

"You promise?"

"Yeah, I promise. Tell me what it is?"

"I can't tell you, I'll have to show you. Follow me but be discreet about it."

They walked across the meadow. Tony stopped by the entrance to his secret place, looked all around to make sure that no one had followed them. When Tony was completely positive that they were alone he pushed back the fence revealing his secret.

"Wow, a secret hideout! Cool!" Sandra said her eyes widening as she looked in.

"Shhh!" Tony said looking round to make sure no one was watching at them and then he ushered her in with a gentle push.

They sat on the floor not knowing what to say to each other. Tony started to crave a smoke and reached over to his tin.

"You smoke?" Tony asked opening the tin and revealing a box of cigarettes which he took out opened and thrust in her direction.

"Yeah," Sandra replied, taking one. "Thanks."

They smoked and discussed the bullies at school Tony found that he actually quite liked Sandra. She wasn't as prim and as innocent as she made herself out to be.

"If only we could get our own back on them." Sandra said.

Tony wriggled a little closer to her, put his arm round her and said, "Maybe I can be of service in that department." He grinned. "But only if you do something in return for me?"

"Okay but what are you going to do?"

"Just wait and see." Tony replied with a glimmer in his eyes.

Just as they stubbed out their cigarettes the school bell rang. As they ran back over to the school building Tony thought about revenge. He'd waited years for this.

Chapter Nineteen

Tony could hear Jackie downstairs. She was beginning to get on his nerves; he didn't like people disturbing his thinking time. He got up off the second hand double bed he'd bought from a junk furniture shop and stomped downstairs. Tony didn't normally spend much time here but with the police still looking for Jackie he couldn't risk being caught at his flat back in Ipswich.

As Tony walked into the room Jackie was still screaming. There were tears streaming down her face.

Tony walked up to Jackie and slapped her hard across the cheek.

"You bastard!" Jackie screamed at him. "Why don't you just kill me now! Or better still give me a knife and I'll do it myself!"

Tony smiled as he felt a movement in his trousers. Jackie was sat on the chair naked her hair was all over the place from earlier on, tears mixed with mascara streaked under her eyes and bruises were breaking out all over her body. Most men would not find that an attractive sight, let alone a turn on but to Tony it was a dream come true and he was getting more and more turned on by the moment. He went round behind her and untied the rope that was attached to the chair.

Jackie started to get up but still weak from her earlier experience, she wasn't quick enough and her knees buckled. Tony picked her up and slung her over his shoulder. She tried to kick him but his grip around her ankles was too tight. He carried her upstairs, opened the bathroom door and dumped her in the bath. He pushed her head under the blood. She could hear him talking. It was muted because of the blood inside her ears but she could just about hear him.

"The more you struggle, the longer your head stays under. Do you understand?" Tony said as lifted her head up.

"You bastard!" She choked.

Tony pushed her head under again. "Do you understand?" He could feel her nodding her head. He let her head up.

She choked a little but didn't say anything.

"Now look what you made me do. I can't clean you off because I would have to empty the bath of all this precious blood I've collected. What to do? What to do?"

Jackie started to whimper.

"Oh don't cry I know what I'll do." He grabbed the rope out of his back pocket, raised her arms and tied her wrists to the shower curtain pole.

Jackie could just feel the bottom of bath with her toes and the stretch on her arms was so intense. She tried to put her feet on the edge of the bath but they kept slipping off making her shoulders feel like they would be pulled from their sockets.

Tony washed the blood from his hands and then started stripping off, pulling his T-shirt over his head and throwing it out the bathroom door into the hallway. Tony undid his jeans and pulled them down, his dick springing up like a clown in a Jack-in-a-box. Throwing his trousers into the hallway to join his T-shirt, he was completely naked.

Tony came over to Jackie, his penis bobbing up and down and placing one hand on each breast he began to lick the blood off her face. Jackie closed her eyes and wished to be somewhere other than here. She could feel his tongue slide over each of her eyelids. His mouth then encircled her nose, sucking gently on it, and then moving slowly down to her lips. His tongue pushed between her lips forcing her mouth open and he groaned. Thinking quickly Jackie bit down hard on his tongue. Tony yelled as best he could with his tongue trapped between her teeth. Jackie could feel the warmth of his fresh blood as it spilled into her mouth. Letting go, she spat it out.

"You bitch!" Tony yelled with a slurred voice. His head came down and he bit her left breast. Jackie could feel his teeth breaking the skin. Tony's hands went down to her thighs and pulled them apart. Jackie screamed as he shoved his dick up and he began pumping hard, pushing it up as far as he could, the end of his dick ramming, pounding into her. He began the licking again, this time more frantic, forgetting the pain of his injured tongue. Every time he got near the wound on her breast, he sucked, taking pleasure in the taste of her blood. He starting grunting, his movements were getting slower but were still as powerful as they were at the start. His grunting got louder as the climax became closer. Sweat started to dot his forehead. Tony started moaning, "Oh Rosie, my beautiful Rosie." Then as Tony climaxed his body became limp, unable to do anymore he fell to the floor, sperm still pumping out the end of his dick.

Tony lay there for quite a while, still grunting and groaning. Looking up at Jackie he could see that she had passed out again, her head had rolled forward so her chin was nearly touching her chest.

When he had regained his strength, he took her downstairs and strapped her back in the chair. Going back upstairs to enjoy the quiet and savour what had happened by writing it all down in his journal.

After logging the past events down, his thoughts returned to Sandra and the revenge on the bullies.

Those were the days. He picked one bully a day to do something awful to. Sometimes he'd do it at school but if he knew where they lived then he'd follow them home and do something there. Once he attached a dead rat to this guy's door and when his mum opened the door in the morning to get the milk in, there it was. Funny thing was, he couldn't remember any of the boy's names, probably because they were insignificant parts of his history.

Anyway, Sandra knew what he was doing but when it came time for her to do him a favour, she wouldn't let him. He guessed that's how all this started.

Tony could still remember how he stuffed one of his sports socks in her mouth to keep her quiet as he enjoyed his first 'real sex' orgasm. It was over and done with quick but then so was Sandra's life.

After Tony realized what he'd done, he didn't know what to do. He ran around his secret place, gathering up his stuff and leaving Sandra on the floor, clothes torn and the sock still in her mouth.

He should've been caught. He would've been caught if they had found her that day. When Tony got home that night, his grandmother wanted his sports clothes to wash. Sorting through he could only find one sock and, panic-stricken, he remembered exactly where he'd left it. Tony told his grandmother that he must have left his socks in the changing room and promptly went outside and burnt the remaining one.

It wasn't until his high school leaving party that Tony had

another 'real woman' sexual experience. Funnily enough, it was with 'Lucy big tits'. She'd had an argument with her date and was sat outside on the school meadow. Tony had been watching what was happening as he had a fag in his secret place. He'd started going back there after all the commotion had died down from the 'Sandra Murder'.

Tony had called to Lucy after the boyfriend had gone. He could hear her crying and still sniffling she came over to him.

"You want a fag?" Tony asked.

"I wouldn't mind." Lucy replied.

"Come on in then." He smiled, pulling back the bush so she could get through easier.

They had talked for a while, him throwing compliment after compliment at her. He kissed her and she seemed to like it so he did it again this time touching her breast at the same time. She moved away saying, "I don't think that we should do this."

"Oh, come on Lucy," he'd said, "I'll just kiss you then. May be we could do it some other time."

He won his argument and began kissing her again. As she started to become more subdued he laid her down on the ground.

She started moaning as he was kissing her and he tried it on again. Finding the bottom of her skirt and pushing his hand up.

"No," She shouted, pushing him off. "You leave me alone or I'll scream."

Tony slapped her hard around the face and Lucy screamed. It was then he lost his patience and punched her straight in the kisser. The impact was such that he knocked her out cold. He started kissing her mouth while ripping the thin straps off her dress. As he kissed her he tasted something sweet. He pulled his head back to look and realized that it was blood from the split lip that he'd given her. Feeling something stirring in his trousers he pulled the top of her dress down revealing her breasts and took a bite. Lucy came round quite suddenly and started to slap him. Fed up with being interrupted, he strangled her.

Her body was found by a man who taking his dog for a walk through the woods. Tony didn't mind, with school now over he no longer needed his secret place. The police never found out who killed her.

After the summer holidays he'd started renting a one

bedroom flat not far from college and that's where he'd met Rose.

He'd met her in the college canteen. Queuing for lunch, they'd both asked for sausage and chips, and there was only one sausage left. Of course being a gentleman he let her have it and that wasn't the only sausage he let her have.

Rose was a lot nicer than any other girl he met. She liked a little rough sex and to start with it was enough to keep him satisfied. Tony forgot about the two girls he'd killed in high school and fell madly in love with her. He'd tried to do his best by her. He'd smartened up when they went to meet her parents. They hadn't liked him from the word go and were adamant that they would never change their minds; giving Rose an ultimatum. Leave him or move out. She moved out and moved in with him.

After about a year their healthy, yet somewhat strange sex life produced a beautiful baby boy. It was after she'd had the baby that she changed her mind, saying that she didn't like sex that way anymore and if he couldn't do it nicely then he couldn't have her. They'd fight when Rose came home from work. He'd accuse her of having affairs and such. Tony would then force himself upon her and spend the rest of the night feeling guilty as listened to her crying herself to sleep. The next day he would always go out and buy her flowers, handing them to her with an apology. She'd accept and they would begin a happy life again. Then it would happen again and the pattern just kept repeating itself until one day she'd run away. Breaking the circle, sending him into depression, and then one day it hit him. He knew just what to do.

Chapter Twenty

Emma sat in her dimly lit living room. She had several candles lit and found it relaxing to watch them stretch and flicker into the darkness. Simply Red's album finally set the peaceful mood. Mick Hucknall's sultry voice singing 'Holding back the years' and as she sunk back into the chair her thoughts changed. She'd started off thinking about her best friend but had somehow ended up on the subject of Steve and 'the kiss'.

All Emma knew is that whenever Steve pulled up outside her heart started beating fast and she wished that he would kiss her again. With Dave, it wasn't like that but he had been so patient and understanding. Did they both still want to be with her? Emma had to decide what she wanted from the both of them. If only Jackie was here, she'd know what to do.

Oh God! Here she was thinking about Dave and Steve and her best friend was possibly dead! Emma knew that she should have kept her big mouth shut. She should have just gone on as if nothing had happened. Everyone said that she was doing the right thing by going to the police, now Emma wished more than anything that she hadn't. In fact she wished that Tony, if that was his real name, had killed her. With that thought she pulled her knees up to her chest and started to cry.

Emma was still like that a half hour later when the doorbell rang. She looked out the window onto the road she saw Steve's car parked by the curb. Her heart stopped for a second and her feet seemed to be rooted to the spot.

It rang again, followed by an urgent knock, which seemed to bring her back down to Earth. She ran to get the door. Her heart was racing, pounding against her chest. Emma felt like she was going to explode as she peered through the spy hole just to see if she was imagining things but she wasn't, there he stood. Emma quickly wiped her tears away and opened the door. As Steve looked straight into her eyes she felt like she was going to melt away.

"Can I come in?" Steve asked, noticing that Emma had been crying.

"Sure. Sorry, I was just surprised to see you here." Emma was reminded of the old saying 'Speak of the Devil and he shall appear' and wondered if it was the same if you were thinking instead of speaking. "Is it news about Jackie?"

"No, I'm sorry nothing yet?" Steve replied. "Has Nick been in touch?"

"No, I was hoping when I saw you that you would have some news. Would you like a coffee?" Emma asked.

"Yeah, that would be great." Steve said.

"Go and make yourself comfy in the living room, I'll bring it through."

Steve wandered off into the living room and Emma headed off to the kitchen.

Putting the kettle on she then leaned on the counter to steady herself. Emma could feel her heart pounding like there was no tomorrow. Secretly, she wished that Steve would kiss her again and again. The more she thought about it, the faster her heart would beat. "Get a grip on yourself woman." She told herself out loud. "Just get a bloody grip on yourself."

"Are you all right?"

Emma leapt like a startled rabbit. "I...I didn't hear you come in." She prayed he hadn't been standing there when she was talking to herself. If he had of seen her he'd probably send for the men in white coats to take her away.

"I was a bit lonely in the living room by myself. Thought I come and keep you company." Steve started to walk towards her.

"Would you like some biscuits with your coffee? Or perhaps you'd like a tea instead?" Emma asked nervously.

"No, coffee will be fine and if you're having biscuits I'll have some but if you're not then don't worry." Steve came up in front of her. "Emma, I can't stop thinking about that kiss the other day. I know you've been thinking about it too." He said leaving out the drunken piece of passion they'd had later on that night. He still wasn't one hundred percent sure if she knew about it or not.

Emma's eyes widened. It was like he was reading her mind. Did he remember what happened after the kiss?

Steve reached out and pushed a loose strand of hair away from her face. "You're so beautiful, you know. I haven't been able to think about anything but you over the past few days. It feels like it was a dream but deep down I know that it wasn't and I want it to be more than a dream. I haven't felt like this about anyone in a long time. I don't know how you feel about me but I'm hoping that it doesn't differ much from my feelings. I care about you a lot, more than you can imagine. I..."

Just then the phone rang interrupting Steve's confession. Emma was too stunned to move so the answer machine got it.

"Hi, it's me Dave. I'm sorry if you're in the bath. Don't get out. I just rang to tell you I'm leaving off in half an hour and I thought I'd pop round to see how you're doing." There was a click as the receiver was put down.

"I guess I'd better go." Steve turned to walk out the kitchen.

"What about your coffee?" Emma asked following him out.

"I'll have it some other time." Steve opened the front door; "I'll speak to you later." He turned and headed down the path.

Emma closed the door and leaned back against it with a big sigh and said to herself. "He didn't give me a chance to tell him I feel the same way." Disappointed she went back into the kitchen and made herself an extra strong cup of coffee.

Dave let himself into Emma's house with the key she'd given him after Jackie had been abducted. He'd been sleeping over a lot since it had happened, so she'd given him a key on the understanding that Dave would call and let her know if he was coming round so she didn't panic when he let himself in.

Dave had been worried about Emma because she hadn't been herself lately. She seemed to be on another planet. Dave knew that she was worried about Jackie but that didn't seem to be the only thing that was on her mind. He was sure that it was more. He thought about asking her but had decided against it. He didn't want to upset her she had enough on her mind. "Hi," Dave shouted as he came in, "Only me."

"Hi." It came from the living room. Dave could see a faint glow of light flicker occasionally. Emma must have her candles lit. He walked into the living room, sat down on the chair beside her and gave her a hug. Despite the dim candlelight Dave could tell that she'd been crying again so held her that little bit tighter. "Jackie will be all right. She's a strong person. She'll be fine, you just wait and see." Dave sounded so reassuring that he was beginning to believe it himself. He felt Emma squeeze him harder and, by that, he knew that his words had done the trick. If only he could make her change her mind about a relationship with him that easily.

Steve went back to his office after speaking to Emma. He knew he really should go home and get some sleep but hell, he was a detective. Detectives didn't need sleep. That was a well-known fact.

Steve started to get the files out on the Rosehill Rapist. If he got caught with the files he'd probably be fired but he had to know what was going on. It didn't matter one iota that he'd been taken off the case, it would always be his and he would be the man to catch the killer!

Steve sat there with the files spread on his desk but it didn't seem to matter how much he immersed himself into his work, he just couldn't stop thinking about Emma. Damn it, why couldn't he stop thinking about her for just one second. She wasn't even his girl for Christ's sakes. Probably wasn't even interested in him anyway. Oh he wanted her to feel the same way about him but he was powerless to do anything about it. Every time he tried Dave would pop up like an unwanted relative over Christmas.

Steve threw the file he was holding down on the desk and walked over to the window. Looking out into the world he found himself distracted by the rain that was dribbling down the windowpane. It was like each drop was in a competition, racing to beat other to the bottom of the window. Racing, reaching the bottom, then having nowhere else to go and nothing else to do. The race was then over, as was their short existence. Had their short life meant anything, changed anything?

Emma stared out of her bedroom window. Dave was asleep downstairs on the sofa bed. She watched the rain trickle down the windowpane and as she drew her attention to her reflection she realized that she couldn't distinguish between the raindrops and her tears.

Chapter Twenty-One

Jackie had been there nine days now and she was feeling very weak. She'd only been given one meal a day, and that wasn't much of a meal. When he'd first tried to feed her she'd refused to eat but by the third day she found the hunger pangs too much to bear. Cold tomato soup wasn't much of a meal but she was grateful of it because when he was feeding her it meant he wasn't raping her.

Jackie had decided that Tony must have a job because after three days of being there all the time he then went to only spending the night there. He arrived around six o'clock and left early in the morning. She also assumed that he had another house, as this one didn't have electricity or gas and he always smelt of aftershave when he came back in the evening.

The sound of the door banging shut made her jump. He was back.

Jackie remembered last night he'd come in, gave her some soup, gagged her and went back out again. It must have been about two hours before he returned. The door woke her then too, and this time he had company.

She could hear them talking in the kitchen.

"Yeah, it's not very nice but my Gran left it for me in her will. I just use it as a place to stay when I visit Ipswich to go clubbing." Jackie noticed that he had made his voice sound different. He sounded like he was from somewhere up north, like Yorkshire. Also, from what he'd told his company, she then deduced that this place was either in or on the outskirts of Ipswich.

"You ought to decorate, it's got potential." Her voice sounded slurred. Mind you, Jackie thought, she had to be drunk to believe that there was potential in this place.

"What's through here?" Jackie saw the door handle move and a crack appeared as the door began to open. Jackie started shouting to try and get some attention but it was hopeless the gag muffled it, making it into a mere grumble.

Tony must have done something because there was a lot of girlish giggles, as the door was pulled closed again, followed by footsteps up the stairs. After a little while the bedsprings started squeaking. Jackie could hear her shouting for more and him grunting. Then suddenly there came a blood-curdling scream.

It had stopped abruptly but Jackie could still hear it in her mind, even now.

Today, Tony came back early wearing a frown. "She's still seeing him!" He yelled at her face as he pulled on a pair of latex gloves, then he reached down and grabbed her necklace, yanking it off from around her neck. He stomped back into the kitchen and came back with a white rosebud and a box. Then he disappeared upstairs for a few minutes, returning with a glass of liquid, which Jackie knew was blood from out of the bath.

Jackie sat there wondering what he was going to do next. She watched as he carefully placed the rosebud and her necklace in the box. Then he picked up the glass and began tipping the blood over the rose and the necklace. When the glass was half empty he stopped.

"What are you doing?" Jackie asked cautiously, not wanting to get him angry.

"It's a present," Tony said smiling, "for Emma. I hope she likes it." He sealed it carefully and picked up the glass of blood. "I propose a toast." He lifted the glass into the air. "To my long life, full of sex, blood and murder, may it never end!" With that, he took a big swallow out of the glass. "Ummm!" He wiped his mouth with the back of his hand.

"Try some." Tony said, walking over and grabbing her by the nose so she couldn't breathe, having then to open her mouth, choking as he poured the blood in.

"I guess it's not *to* everyone's taste!" He laughed, picking up the box and leaving.

As soon as Tony had closed the back door, Jackie began to struggle with the ropes that bound her wrists together. Knowing it was futile but with the thought of Ipswich being not far from where she was she felt she had to try. The ropes made her wrists burn with pain as they rubbed deeper into the sores that they themselves had formed over the past nine days. Tears sprung into Jackie's eyes as she thought of Emma receiving that box and making assumption that Tony had killed her. That thought installed a new fear and made her feel sick to the pit of her stomach. If Emma thought she was already dead, then Tony would have no need to keep her around. She had to escape, because next time he came back, he'd kill her.

Jackie looked around, her attention drawn to the kitchen. The glass that Tony had used for the blood was stood on the worktop by the sink. If she could just get into the kitchen maybe then she could knock the glass off the work top and get a piece sharp enough to cut the rope that bound her wrists and the chair together. It sounded impossible but she had to try.

Jackie tried to lift the chair but it was too awkward to do for too long. So she let it drop to the floor and started to drag it across the room instead. It made a really loud screeching sound as it scraped against the floor. Despite all the noise it made, Jackie could still hear her heart thumping as it felt as if it wanted to break free of her chest and run away from this without her.

Suddenly, Jackie came to abrupt halt as the chair caught in the doorway on the shallow step. With all of her strength she lifted the chair over the step and began dragging it across the kitchen floor to the sink.

When Jackie got to the sink she tried to knock the glass into it. Instead, it fell to the floor, shattering into hundreds of tiny pieces on the tiles. Then Jackie noticed that a draw to the left of the sink had been had been left slightly open. When she looked in she saw a large knife. It was the most beautiful knife she'd ever seen. The blade was about eight inches long and it had an intricately carved handle with a white stone placed in it just before the blade started. It had to be worth a fortune. Jackie grabbed the drawer between her teeth and pulled it open until it came out, bounced off her knees and fell to the floor with a earth-shattering bang.

"This is going to hurt." Jackie said to herself, as she rocked the chair from side to side. When it had gained enough momentum she fell to the floor.

"Oomph!"

Jackie slid herself and the chair across the floor to where the knife had landed, trying not to go through too much of the glass. Glass being the least of her worries if she was caught trying to escape.

Backing up to the knife Jackie grasped in one hand and began to rub it against the ropes. Jackie felt it catch her skin a couple of times but then felt the ropes loosen as they did she was able to pull the rope until it snapped and she was free. Relief took over as Jackie slowly stood up, tears started to flow as she rubbed her sore wrists. She noticed had a few nicks on them but they weren't bleeding too badly.

Next, she needed some clothes. Jackie headed upstairs; he must have some clothes somewhere. She decided to look in the other bedroom upstairs. She knew that there wasn't any in the bathroom or bedroom she'd already been in.

As Jackie opened the door to the other room she prepared herself for what she might see. The window of this room was also boarded up and by the amount of light that was coming through the cracks in the boards Jackie could tell that the sun was on its way down. She had to hurry, looking over in the corner Jackie could see a body slumped up against the wall. Hurrying over to it, not knowing whether it would have clothes on, she tripped and landed on something soft. As she looked at it, realizing it was another body and stifled back a scream. Maybe this was the girl he'd killed last night.

Jackie grabbed some of the clothes that were lying around the body and put them on. They didn't fit too well but she didn't have time to search for her own which she knew were probably round here somewhere, at least they covered her a bit though. The shoes didn't fit at all. Jackie went over to the other body but it was so stiff that she couldn't get the shoes off its feet. Bare foot would have to do.

Hurrying back downstairs and into the kitchen, she noticed by the drawer lay a book. It looked really worn and Jackie didn't know why but she picked it up and opened it. Looking through the pages she saw it was a diary.

10th October 1987

Drove down to the whore district last night. Picked up a whore called Candy (I don't think that was her real name). Took her back to the pad that I bought a last month. Tried to have normal sex with her. She started to laugh when I couldn't perform. So I slapped that stupid smile of her face. I started to get really aroused, so I just kept on hitting her. Then I rammed my dick into her so hard it's a wonder I couldn't see it at the back of her throat when she screamed. The more she shouted and screamed, the more I got turned on. I reached for my knife and began stabbing her. Her screaming turned into gurgling as the blood oozed out of her mouth. I kissed her, licking up the blood. It tasted so sweet. It was then I had my best ever orgasm. I had fun dismantling her body this morning. Put the pieces in the spare room. I ate the kidneys for dinner. Decided to do this again, maybe I could do it with Rosie if she doesn't want to

Jackie couldn't believe what she was reading. It was like an extract from a horror story. This sort of thing didn't happen, well maybe in the America but not in England. He'd obviously murdered more people than the police thought. She grabbed the diary and pen, and headed for the back door.

Knowing that she didn't have much time or any money, Jackie had to think fast. She had to get this book to the police and tell him where his hide out was but it wouldn't be long before Tony came back to find her gone.

As Jackie hurried up the road, not knowing where she was or where she was going she spotted a moped across the street and headed towards it. Somebody must live in the house that it was parked outside.

Jackie walked up to the front door. She could hear the bell ring, pressing it several times but no one came to the door. Jackie ripped out a page from the diary and wrote down the house number and the registration of the motorcycle, she'd record the road name when she got to the end where the sign was usually located. Jackie placed the paper in her pocket. Then she wrote on the front of the book, 'Please take this to Detective Harris at Ipswich police station,' and posted it through the letterbox.

Walking away from the house, Jackie looked down the road to house where she'd been imprisoned for the last nine days and hoped that she was heading in the right direction.

Chapter Twenty-Two

It was dark now and Jackie had given up running ages ago. Her feet were sore from the bits on the road and she was still a bit out of breath but despite this she carried on walking. The houses had finished ages ago, she tried all the doors but it was like a ghost town. Nobody seemed to be in. All Jackie had around her now was fields and bushes, and she still didn't know whether she was going the right way. Jackie looked down the road back the way she'd just come. Her heart sunk. Maybe she'd decided on the wrong way after all.

As Jackie carried on walking she spotted a sign post up ahead. Getting closer she could see it said Ipswich 3 miles. She was nearly there. Who was she kidding, three miles! She already felt like she'd walked a million. At least she was out of that hell house now. Slumping down on the grass verge Jackie thought. 'I'll just have a quick rest.'

Emma opened the door to find a parcel sitting on her doorstep.

"Who is it?" Dave yelled from the living room.

"Just a parcel." Emma said puzzled but in a way, knowing what it was. She sat on the chair opposite Dave and opened it slowly, not really wanting to look inside. A look of despondency appeared on her face as she looked into the box. Turning to Dave Emma quietly said, "Jackie's dead."

Jackie awoke as a car passed by her, headlights glaring into the darkness. She didn't know how long she'd been asleep and as she moved she felt the coldness of the evening air envelope her. Shivering, Jackie stood up and started walking again. Her feet were freezing and ached from all the miles she'd already walked.

Hunched over and feeling ready to give up, a car passed by, headlights glaring, making her momentarily blind in the darkness but giving light to her thoughts. Maybe she could thumb a lift. Jackie knew how dangerous hitchhiking could be but she had to take a chance. She was so tired and she had to get to Detective Harris as soon as she could.

Steve followed Dave into the living room where Emma sat staring out of the window. Steve could see she'd been crying but she still looked beautiful, despite the red eyes and nose.

"What's happening?" Dave asked, "Did you get anything off the box?"

"Well, the only prints were there from the kid who delivered it. He said that a man fitting Tony's description gave him a fiver to put the package on your doorstep, ring the doorbell and run off."

"What about the blood in the box?" Emma asked.

"Well Forensics ran some tests on it. It's definitely human but these things take time." Steve explained.

"Well, at least there's still a chance that Jackie may be alive."

Dave said, trying to make Emma think positive, which was hard when he wasn't thinking positive himself.

"No," Emma said, "she's not alive, he's killed her. Jackie's dead and it all my fault." She got up and walked out of the room.

Jackie ran to the car and got in. It was the first car that had stopped since she started thumbing. She was beginning to wonder whether anyone was going to stop. It was understandable though, looking at the state of her, they probably thought that she was a tramp or a gypsy.

Jackie climbed in, closed the door and put her seat belt on. "Thank you very much for stopping." She said politely, "I must get to Ipswich Police Station. It's really urgent." She turned to look at the driver and screamed.

Panicking, Jackie tried to get the door open but as she fumbled with the handle Tony took a monkey wrench from the behind the seat, bringing it down on the top of her head and knocking her out.

"So you thought you could get away from me, did you?"

Tony sneered, "Well you thought wrong. Why couldn't you have just been a good girl? Why did you have to make trouble for yourself? I didn't really want to kill you. I was actually getting to like having you around but now I'll have to kill you for real. You really have spoilt my plans."

Two days after Emma had received Jackie's necklace in a box she opened the door to find a deliveryman holding another small box.

"Sign here please Miss." He said handing her the clipboard.

Emma took it, signed her name and swapped it for the parcel.

Emma went into the sitting room and put the parcel on the table. She already knew who it was from. It was getting to be a routine. Emma also knew that she didn't want to open it. Maybe she should wait until Dave came round after work. Maybe she should call Steve and let him know that she'd received another package. Fighting with herself she finally opened the card attached to the box. It said,

Emma, curiosity getting the best of her, peeled back the parcel tape that held the lid down, opened the flaps and slowly peered into the box. Emma jumped up from the chair, sending the box flying and ran into the kitchen retching. She could feel her stomach churning, her meagre breakfast bubbling its way up and finally projecting itself into the sink.

As soon as she'd washed her mouth out with some water the phone rang. She let the answer machine get it.

"I know you're there Emma." said the voice that she had come to dread. "Hope you liked my present. Well, it wasn't really from me. As you can see, Jackie loved you with all of her heart." Laughing, he put the receiver down.

Emma ran over to the answer machine, picked it up and threw it across the room at the wall. The phone then rang again. Picking up the receiver this time, she cautiously said, "Hello."

"Emma, are you all right?" It was Steve.

"Yes, I'm fine and the cat's still smiling."

Steve noticed from the way her voice quivered when Emma spoke that not everything was all right. "Look, I'm coming over, see you in a few minutes."

Emma sat in the kitchen until Steve arrived, not wanting to go back in the living room where the box was. Emma answered the door telling Steve immediately to go in the living room and look in the box on the floor. Steve stifled back the urge to throw up. He couldn't believe his eyes.

"It's Jackie's heart," Emma said from the doorway. "He sent it to me. I can't take much more of this Steve, it's driving me crazy." She started to cry and pace up and down the hallway like a bear in a small cage.

Walking towards her, Steve said, "I know. I know." And he put his arms around Emma to make her feel better, holding her tight, he found it felt really good for him too. It felt so good that he wished that it didn't have to end as Emma pulled away from him slightly. She looked up at him with those beautiful big hazel eyes full of tears. Steve knew it was against regulations to get involved with someone whose case he was working on but hell the Super had taken him off the case now. The last time he had kissed her he could put it down to drunkenness or stress but this time there was no excuse. Emma had driven him mad since the day he first set eyes on her at the hospital. Rules were the last thing on his mind at the moment. Just as he brought his head down to kiss her his C.B. sprung into action.

"Excuse me." Steve said and feeling cheated again he went off into the living room, leaving Emma feeling totally bewildered.

When he came back into the hallway a moment later he was looking very pale and carrying the box. "Got to go, I'll speak to you later ok."

Chapter Twenty-Three

Steve burst into the Supers office, "Bill, you've got to let me back on the case. I'm the best chance you've got at catching this killer. Nick Fisher's a good bloke but he's never going to catch him. Let me back I'm begging you!"

"I can't Steve. You're too involved." Bill said.

"I'm not interested in Emma." Steve lied, "And even if I was I wouldn't let it blur my judgment. Bill you've known me for years and you know that I give one hundred and ten percent to my job. You've got to let me back. I can catch this man, I know I can."

Bill looked Steve straight in the eye, "Nick Fisher is on the case and that's final."

Steve threw the box with Jackie's heart on Bill's desk and headed to the door. "This is what happens when you take your best man off the case!" Slamming the door behind him he headed to his office.

Dave came home to a very quiet house. As he walked through to the sitting room he saw Emma standing and staring out the window. He walked over to her and sat down. "Are you all right?" he asked putting his arm around her shoulders.

"Jackie's dead." She said quietly.

"I thought we spoke about this the other day. It was just her necklace; it doesn't mean that he's killed her. There's still a chance."

"I received another parcel today." Emma explained. "It had a heart in it. Her heart."

"Are you sure it was hers?" Dave asked. "I mean he'd already sent you her necklace and as far as Forensics were concerned the blood wasn't hers. It could be a heart from the butchers or something."

"Forensics are positive that it's a human heart and the blood type matched Jackie's."

Dave was concerned about the way Emma had detached herself from what was going on. "Look, I'm going to call Geoff and tell him I can't come in tonight."

"No," Emma said, "you go to work. I need to be by myself and besides Geoff will need you in. He's already down two members of staff."

"Don't be stupid. I don't think you should be by yourself at the moment and it's not that busy on a Tuesday anyway."

"Look, Dave," Emma said shrugging his arm off her shoulders and getting up. "I feel crowded. I need time to take in what has happened and..."

"What are you trying to say?" Dave asked. "All the time you've been asking for company saying that you don't want to be alone. Are you now saying that you don't want me around anymore?"

"No," Emma replied, "I just need a little space. A lot has happened and I need time to get my head round it all. I think you should back off for a while. Give me some space. Maybe, you should stop staying round here for a bit..."

Dave didn't give her time to finish what she was saying, he got up, grabbed his bag out of the bathroom and left.

Emma didn't go after him. Even if she dare leave the house, she knew that Dave would be in no mood to talk with her. Maybe once he'd finished work tonight and had time to think about it he'd see sense.

Steve pulled up behind the police car that was parked on the road by the field and turned on his hazard lights. They'd had a call at the station from a farmer. He'd said a couple walking their dogs had come across a body on his land. Steve instinctively knew it had to be Jackie's. He also knew that he shouldn't be here and as he walked over to the two very pale looking policemen, Steve really wished he could have prevented this. "You all right guys?" He asked.

"Yes Sir." They said simultaneously.

"It's a bit bad Sir." The young one added, "Freddie Krueger couldn't have made a better job of it."

Steve followed the younger one to where the body was. He took one look at it and turned away, coughing into the sleeve of his coat. If this *were* Jackie they would need dental records to confirm it!

After he'd got over the initial shock, he started to take notes on the scene. Our murderer had been very busy, mutilating the body beyond recognition, removing all the organs. Why had he done this? He knew that we would know straight away who it was, so why go to all that extra effort?

The body had been strung up on the existing scarecrow pole. He'd placed the scarecrows head where the victims should be and then placed the victims head on the floor looking up at the body. The eyes had been ripped out and placed in a group with the other organs. These were neatly laid out around the body. Her intestines had been hung around the neck like a garland of death. He'd certainly had the time to play about.

After looking at all the organs, he found that the heart was missing. This confirmed that the body had to be Jackie's. All that was needed now was a blood test but Steve knew it would only be done to confirm what they already knew. It was Jackie all right.

This was the worst butchering that Steve had ever seen but if this had happened here where was the blood? There should have been more blood. It was obvious that Jackie had been mutilated somewhere else. The question was where?

"Okay boys, take some pictures." Steve said, holding back

his emotions, and his need to be sick. He didn't know how he was going to tell Emma what had happened. As he started to walk away from the scene, he saw Bill and Nick talking. He tried to sneak back to his car without them noticing, when he was stopped in his tracks by a familiar voice, "Harris! I want to see you back at my office pronto!"

The doorbell rang at about eight-thirty. Emma wondered who it could be. Maybe Dave hadn't gone into work and despite what had been said he'd come round to keep her company.

Emma looked through the peephole. It was Steve. Her heart skipped a beat. What was he doing round here? He hadn't called to say he was coming. Emma took a quick look at herself in the mirror and wished she hadn't because she looked like hell.

Steve rang the doorbell again. What was taking her so long, he thought? He wished she'd hurry up; he wanted to get this over and done with before Nick made it round here and Bill realised where he had gone before going to his office. Steve knew that it was going to hit her hard, even though Emma thought knew what had happened, this was just going to prove that she was right because while there was no proof then there was still a small chance that it hadn't happened.

Emma opened the door and smiled. Steve walked in and Emma knew something was wrong. He didn't smile back. As she was about to ask him what was wrong, the telephone rang. Emma picked up the receiver and Steve moved in close so he could listen into the call.

"Hello Emma." Tony said sounding pleased with himself. "It's nice to see the Detective round there with you again. I gave him a lovely surprise today. Why don't you ask him about it? Tell him not to leave out the gory details. Just mention Jackie." The machine clicked off as he put the receiver down. Emma, stood there unable to move to put the receiver back on the cradle, with tears welling in her eyes looked questionably at Steve.

"You'd better sit down." Steve said sitting on the sofa and patting the cushion beside him. Steve told Emma that they'd found Jackie's body, he didn't tell her how he'd found it, he just explained that it was in a bad way.

Tears started to roll down Emma's face, and Steve pulled her to him. He liked the way she fitted snugly in his arms. He pressed his face into her hair it smelt so sweet. He just had to kiss her, just once, with no interruptions, no phone ringing. Just the two of them and then she'd know just how much he'd fallen for her. She'd know that he wanted to take care of her. Protect her from this vile man. He lifted her chin so she was looking up at him and brought his lips down to meet hers.

As soon as they'd touched, Emma felt as if she'd been taken to another place. Away from the madness of this world to some place where there was no murder, no killing, no sadness, a place of happiness, love and romance.

So carried away with the moment were they that they never heard the door open as Dave, on a break, popped by to see how Emma was doing. They failed to notice until a voice said, "So you need time on your own!" and this was followed by the door slamming as a disgruntled Dave left.

Emma pulled herself away from Steve and ran to the window just in time to see Dave running down the street.

"Oh God," Emma cried. "I've got to go after him and explain."

"I'll go after him." Steve said, "You stop here. I'll be back in a minute."

"But Steve," Emma started, "he isn't going to listen to you."

"He'll have to. I can't have you running around out there. The fact that Tony knows I'm here means he could be around the corner waiting for you to do just that." And with that he'd ran out the front door, talking into his CB, asking for all cars to be on the lookout.

It was half an hour before Steve returned. Emma had been going out of her mind with worry. When she opened the door and saw that Dave wasn't with him she said, "He's dead too, isn't he?"

Steve looked at her, "What makes you say that. He probably just needs to be by himself at the moment."

"He's going to kill everyone that has connection with me. It's the only way he can hurt me. He can't kill me, so he's going to make my life miserable."

"Look, I've got all cars looking out for him, it's the best I can do."

Just then his CB came to life. He went out into the hallway.

A few minutes later he came back in, "I've got some good news." He said smiling.

"Have they found Dave?" Emma asked.

"No but I am sure he can look after himself. They found a piece of notepaper in the side of Jackie's mouth. It has a registration number on it. They're tracing it now. This is it Emma, we've got him now."

Dave sat down on a bench by the side of the docks. It was dark but the moon was full and it lit up the night sky just enough to see. He'd been walking for what seemed like an eternity after he finally ran out of energy to run. Every time Dave had stopped, thinking he was alone, he'd suddenly find there were people everywhere. Couples would appear out of the woodwork walking hand in hand and kissing. All he wanted was to be alone with his thoughts.

Finally he'd found somewhere he could be alone. Dave lit up a cigarette and looked into the water. The ripples glimmered in the moonlight where the fish were coming up to eat insects on the water's surface. It was very peaceful. He could hear the chirping of crickets in the long grass behind him and the odd splash of a fish jumping from the water to catch flying insects from the air.

Why had Emma done this to him? He thought. How could she? It was obvious that the killer knew more about her than he did. Dave knew that Emma and Steve had become close over the past few months but he didn't think that they'd become that close. Emma had always maintained that she wasn't ready to start a relationship. That was a lie. Why couldn't she have just said that she didn't want a relationship with him? Instead she'd let him keep on hoping that there was still a chance and that he'd just have to take it steady with her. He felt a fool for believing her and not going with what his instincts were telling him.

Footsteps interrupted his thoughts. A man in a scruffy overcoat approached him.

"Excuse me," He said politely, "do you have a light?"

"Yeah." Dave said, turning away from the man and fumbling in his coat pocket for his lighter.

"That's okay, I've found mine." The man said and he suddenly hurled himself straight at Dave.

Dave turned back to face the man, shocked to see that he was coming straight at him out of the darkness wielding a knife. Before he could do anything the man began stabbing him.

The pain was terrible. Dave could feel the knife penetrating his stomach, his chest, the repeated plunging in and dragging out making him feel weak. Dave tried to fight but as the blood began blocking his windpipe he found hard to breathe and started choking, each intake of air sent pains into his lungs. Eventually though, the pain was started to slowly fade away. This was followed by a blackness that was darker than the night. In the distance he could see a vibrant light he made his way toward it. It was drawing him to it like a peaceful, magnetic force. With peace in mind, he let himself go.

Steve walked into Bill's office after being summoned for the second time today. Steve knew by the look on Bill's face as he entered that he was in deep shit.

"Where have you been, I told you immediately?" Bill snapped.

"I had something to take care of first." Steve replied.

"I bet you did!" Bill replied, "I don't know what the hell you think you're up to going down to a murder scene of the case I explicitly said you were off. You got a nerve disobeying my orders."

"Sorry Bill."

"Anyway, you're back on the case."

"What?" Steve said disbelieving what his ears were telling him.

"You're back on the case. Now get out of my sight!"

"Thanks Bill." Steve said as he hurried out the office.

Tony laughed as he pushed the body into the river. He threw the long scabby coat in after it. "Two down, one to go!" He said to himself. Tony smiled as he thought about how his brilliant plan had worked. He'd known that if he phoned Dave up and told him that Emma was having an affair with Detective Harris, he'd go running to her house to confront her. Tony had seen Harris arrive but he didn't know that there actually was something going on between them. Obviously, now that he knew there was something going on he'd have to kill Harris for laying his hands on her. She was his after all but it was funny how they just happened to be kissing when Dave walked through the door. Brilliant timing, he thought, laughing as he walked away with Dave's keys in his hand.

Chapter Twenty-Four

Detective Harris had been up this road before. It was where they had found the fifth body and here he was at the house of the man who had found that body. Who would have thought it, the man who found the fifth victim was the murderer. A good way of getting yourself off the list of suspects, by pretending to have found the body! Two policemen stood behind him, ready to chase should the suspect decide to flee. They'd looked up the registration and it had come up with the name Carl Jackson. Steve thought that maybe the name Tony was an alias. He couldn't believe that Carl Jackson was the killer. He didn't seem to fit the killer profile or Emma's description but Steve had to go along with the evidence that they'd found on Jackie's body. To Steve, he had seemed so normal when they'd questioned him about his discovery of the fifth body but in this job, normal from outside appearances didn't always mean normal on the inside. Who knows what goes on inside the mind of an average looking man?

The door opened slowly and a very tired looking man said, "How can I help you? Oh, Detective Harris, how are you?"

"Mr Carl Jackson," Steve said, "I'm placing you under arrest for the kidnap and murder of Miss Jackie Summers. Anything you say will be taken down and used as evidence against you. Do you understand?"

"No! I don't know what you're talking about? I haven't murdered anyone!"

The two policemen grabbed his arms and led him down to the police car.

Steve pushed the record button on the tape and said, "For the tape it's ten minutes past ten on the morning of February the fourth. Conducting the interrogation are myself Detective Steve Harris and Detective Nick Fisher. Brought in for interrogation is Mr Carl Jackson who is suspected of the kidnap and murder of

Miss Jackie Summers."

Emma entered Ipswich Police Station. She felt incredibly nervous. She didn't really want to go through with this. Emma didn't know what she'd do when she saw him but she was shaking like a leaf already.

Steve had called her in to identify him because they couldn't get him to confess. All he kept saying was that he didn't know anything about a murder or a rape. He didn't know anyone called Jackie Summers.

Steve had noticed that Emma was upset about having to identify him and said, "Don't worry, he won't be able to see you, you'll be behind a one way mirror, you can see him but all he can see is himself. You just have a really good look and tell us if you can see him in the line up. Okay?"

"Okay." Emma said quietly.

They entered the room, which was lit only by a small, dim light and Steve closed the door. Emma looked closely at the men on the other side of the glass. She turned to Steve, her eyes bleary with tears, "He's not there. Tony's not there."

"Are you sure?" Steve asked, confused. He couldn't believe that this man wasn't the killer. They'd found a diary at his house describing details to all the murders, details that the only the police new about.

"I'm sure." Emma said.

"Okay." Steve said, "I'll arrange for Detective Thompson to take you home and stay with you until further notice." Now all he had to do was find out why this man had the killer's diary and why the note of his license plate number was in Jackie's possessions when she was murdered.

Emma opened the door to her house. She was glad to be back inside. She felt safe inside knowing that she could lock the doors and Tony couldn't get her.

"How long are you going to be here?" Emma asked,

"I don't know," said Detective Thompson. "As long as they need me here, now that Harris is back on the case he wants someone in the house with you until they catch the guy."

"Would you like some coffee?" Emma asked.

"Yes please. Err...where is your toilet?"

"Upstairs, first on the right." Emma said as she walked into the kitchen.

As he stood in front of the toilet, whistling to drown out the noise of him peeing, he felt something tickle the back of his neck. He looked to see what it was. There was nothing there. He returned back to his business. It was then he felt a sharp pain in his back and a voice said, "Direct hit." Detective Thompson slumped to the floor.

"Do you take sugar or milk?" Emma shouted up from the bottom of the stairs.

"No, neither."

Emma went back in the kitchen and put the mugs coffee and a plate of biscuits on a tray. She walked into the hallway towards the living room door and kicked it open. The floor of the living room was covered in white roses. Dropping the tray, Emma ran upstairs to get Detective Thompson.

Emma knocked on the bathroom door. "Detective Thompson." There was no answer. She tried to push open the door but something was stopping it. Emma slowly put her head round the door and saw the detective slumped up against the wall, blood spreading out around him like lava flowing from a volcano. Emma stifled a scream and went to run downstairs but there, standing at the bottom was Tony.

"Hello Rosie." He said grinning from ear to ear. He pulled a bloodied knife from behind his back and started slowly coming towards her up the stairs.

Emma ran into her bedroom, locking the door behind her and diving across the bed for the phone, she picked it up and began to dial out. Nothing happened. No tone. The line was dead.

Emma opened the window and for one insane minute she considered jumping then leaving the window, she moved over to the built in wardrobe and opened the door.

"Come on Rosie," Tony yelled, "open the door. I won't hurt you. I promise."

Emma shoved the shoes across the bottom of the wardrobe, crouched down inside and closed the door behind herself. "Please God," she asked quietly, "Don't let him find me." Emma could feel herself trembling and her heart was beating so loud that it could probably heard streets away. Tears began to roll down her cheeks and she began to think about what he would do if he found her?

"Come on Rosie, I won't hurt you, just be a good girl and open the door." His voice sounded sinister.

Emma crouched in the cupboard, trying not to make a noise, trying to hold her breath so he wouldn't hear her. She wondered why he was calling her Rosie again. Who was this Rosie person? Was this Rosie the cause of all this trouble? Tony was clearly insane but why? Had this Rosie person hurt him? Had she driven him to do this?

"If you don't open this door soon, I'll break it down." Tony shouted, "I won't be happy if I have to do that Rosie. You know what happens if I'm not happy." His voice suddenly changed from angry to pleading, like he was playing 'good guy, bad guy' all by himself. "I don't want to hurt you Rosie but if you make me break down this door then I have to punish you to teach you a lesson. I love you Rosie, don't make me hurt you."

Steve sat in his office with Detective Nick Fisher reading some of the extracts out of the diary. They couldn't believe what they were reading. Tony had murdered so many women, most of which the police didn't even know about.

The only ones that they knew about were the four that Tony had believed were his ex-wife Rose, the call girl that his diary mentioned had nearly got away and Steve's ex-wife Mary along with his latest victim, Jackie.

"So, that was the reason he carved Rose across the victims abdomens." Nick said.

"Rose had left him and he wanted her back." Steve stated, "So he went looking for her and only found women who resembled her."

"And believing they were her he raped and killed them. If he couldn't have her then no one could have her." Nick finished for him.

"Tony had written everything down in his diary as an account of what had happened. How he'd stalk his victims for weeks sometimes months before he raped and killed them, all the meticulous planning that went into stalking them and then finally killing them in just the right way." Steve said.

"What about the one's that didn't look like Rose?" Nick asked.

"It looks like he chose those victims purely to satisfy his sexual needs. Those were the ones that he'd take back to his house and kill."

Tony had written everything in so much detail that they knew the dates, places and even some of the times of the murders. The only thing he hadn't put down was the address of the house that they were being taken back to. Steve had a gut feeling that it couldn't be too far from Mr Jackson's house.

"We need to get some officers to go down to where Mr Jackson lives for a good nose around. That house has got to be around there somewhere." Steve said to Nick.

Just then the door to his office opened. "Inspector Harris, Sir, we've got another dead body." The young officer blurted out. "It's just been found in the River Orwell, not far from the docks. It got caught up in a boy's fishing line. The officer at the scene seems to think that it could be the male friend of the rape victim."

Steve jumped up from his chair and grabbed his coat. He turned to Nick, "Organize officers to look round near the Jackson house and then start a search for this Rose woman that's in the diary. She is our key to finding Tony."

"Okay Rosie, I'm breaking down the door." Tony shouted.

Emma jumped and whimpered when she heard the first thud against the bedroom door. She reached down beside her and grabbed a shoe, holding it ready to throw if he opened the cupboard door. It was stupid place to hide, she thought, it will be the first place he looks. She should have taken the chance and jumped out of the window. Maybe she'd have broken and arm or a leg but she'd be out of the house and someone would have seen her. She could've screamed to get someone's attention.

Just then Emma heard a long cracking noise followed by a deafening bang as the lock on the door gave way and hit the wall of the built in wardrobe where she was hiding. Emma jumped, a scream very nearly escaped from between her lips and she covered her mouth with her hand. Biting her tongue, Emma tried not to give her hiding place away with an accidental whimper.

It was just starting to get dark again when Steve got to the murder site. Despite his face being wrinkled from the water, as soon as they had uncovered the head of the dead man he knew it was Dave. Steve didn't know how he was going to tell Emma. Why couldn't he have just listened to her? He should have protected both Jackie and Dave and now they were dead. Was Tony going to kill everyone who was close to Emma or was it just because both Jackie and Dave had seen him? That didn't explain why he had killed Mary but he had a feeling he knew why Tony had done that.

Emma could hear Tony's footsteps as he entered the bedroom.

"Where are you hiding Rosie?" His footsteps quickened away from the wardrobe. "So you've jumped out the window."

Emma heard the window close, followed by quick footsteps and the bedroom door slamming shut. Relief came over her and Emma let out a sigh as she stopped holding her breath. Still gripping the shoe she got up slowly to leave the wardrobe and make her escape. Emma reached for the handle of the door but before she could grip it the door opened and the handle swung out of reach.

Emma screamed and threw the shoe at Tony. It bounced off his shoulder like a stuffed toy.

Tony grabbed Emma's arm and pulled her out of the wardrobe and swung her onto the bed.

Landing on her front, Emma tried to crawl away pulling at the covers. Tony clambered on top of her legs and shoved a handkerchief into her face. Chloroform. This was new to Tony but he didn't want to hurt her and after a while she started to go limp. As soon as Tony felt he could, he moved off and started tying her up.

Looking outside he could see that darkness had fell. Now was the time. He quickly wrapped her up in a blanket and carried her out to his car.

Chapter Twenty-Five

Steve pulled up outside Emma's house. Something wasn't right. There were no lights on. Steve got out of his car and ran up the steps to the front door. As he went to knock on the door it started slowly opening.

Tony drove slowly past his house. There were two police cars and a van parked outside. They were bringing out a body bag and put it into the back of the van. How had they found this place? Nobody who was alive knew about it. He'd have to take Rosie back to their old flat. Tony really wanted to show her the new home that he bought for them to live in. Angry that his dream family home had been found, Tony headed back to Ipswich to the tiny one-bedroom flat.

Steve walked into the living room and turned on the light. "Oh my god." He gasped as he saw the living room floor. There were white roses everywhere. A tray had been dropped and the mugs lay on the floor beside it. Tony had been here.

Steve checked the kitchen, nothing out of place in there. Turning on the hall lights he headed up the stairs. He noticed the blood that was seeping from under the bathroom door. Pushing it slowly open as far as it would go he put his head round. "Thompson." He yelled. He pushed his way into the room and check Thompson for a pulse. He knew before he did that was too late and that Thompson had been dead long before he got here.

Steve ran round the house frantically looking for Emma but she wasn't there. When he looked in her bedroom he could see that there had been a struggle. The wardrobe door was open and the sheets on the beds were all screwed up.

Steve looked around but there were no traces of blood. 'Then there's still a chance that she's alive.' He thought, wishing that he'd never called off the surveillance but he'd felt sure that they had the right man. He headed back to his car and drove back to the station.

Emma dreamt that she was stuck in quick sand. She couldn't move her arms or legs. Everyone was just standing around, watching her sink. "Help me." She asked the people in her dream. Emma could see Jackie and Dave standing by a palm tree drinking out of coconuts that had straws and little umbrellas sticking out the top. She saw Steve was laughing and pointing at her.

"Please help me Steve." Emma said confused as to why he was laughing at her. He didn't help her; he just turned his back on her and ordered a drink from the bar.

"Why won't you help me," she screamed out loud waking herself up.

Emma looked around. Where was she? Was she at home? It didn't feel like home. It didn't smell like home. It was very dark and she couldn't see a thing. Still feeling groggy, she suddenly remembered Tony being at her house. She was struggling on the bed with him. He had covered her nose and mouth with something and then she felt sleepy and weak.

It felt like she was on a bed but it didn't feel like her bed. Emma tried to move but her arms and legs appeared to be tied to something.

Suddenly the light came on. Emma, blind for a moment, blinked several times, trying to get her eyes accustomed to the sudden glare. Once she'd got used to the light, Emma could see that Tony had stripped her down to her underwear and then tied her wrists and ankles to the bedposts.

"How are you feeling?" Tony said from his chair in the corner of the room. "It's been lovely to watch you sleeping. Did you have a nightmare? I hope you did because that's what you've turned my life into! Since you left me my life has been a living hell! And now I'm going to do the same to yours!" He shouted standing up. He started to pace along the bottom of the bed.

Emma lifted her head, looked him straight in the eyes and shouted, "Well go on then! Kill me! Just get it over and done with! I don't know why you didn't just kill me down that alley!"

"I couldn't have done that Rosie and I'm not going to do it now. You're special, not like that slut Jackie. You deserve better than I did to her. I'm not going to kill you just yet. Firstly though, I need some answers. I need to know what you've done with my baby boy?"

"Look, my name's not Rosie its Emma and I don't know anything about a damn baby!" She shouted almost spitting with rage and not knowing how she'd suddenly become so brave but maybe it was because she didn't care.

Tony walked quickly over her and slapped her round the face. Then he sat down beside her on the bed. "You'll be a good girl from now on, won't you Rosie? You're not going to leave me again, are you?" He said producing a knife. "I'm going to make sure of that."

Emma shook her head. She could feel her cheek stinging and burning hot from where his hand had made an impact.

She looked nervously around the bedroom. It was sparsely furnished with just a bed, a chair, a wardrobe and a cot. The wallpaper had little orange and pink rosebuds making it a cosy little room, not the sort you would expect a killer to own.

Tony grabbed her face and turned it to look at him. "You know what will happen if you try to leave me don't you?" Tony said caressing her neck with the cold knife blade and then as if to prove a point he slid it carefully down the valley between her breasts, severing the thin strip of lace that connected the cups of her bra. "That's better." He smiled and delicately placed a kiss on one of her breasts.

Frozen in fear, like a mouse under attack, Emma lay there like she was dead.

Steve walked into Nick Fishers office. "Have you found that Rose woman yet?"

"Yes, she'd changed her name when she left Tony and she moved to Cambridge with a friend, so it took me a while to find out her new name and where she'd moved to. She left Tony because he used to beat her up and force himself sexually upon her. Anyway, she told me all this on the phone and she's offered to help us find him. We've got a car on its way to pick her up now. Also we've found the house. The team has nicknamed it the 'Slum of Slaughter'. It's unbelievable what they've found in there…"

"Very tactful." Steve interrupted. "Tony's got Emma. We need to find out where he's taken her. He obviously hasn't taken her to the 'Slum of Slaughter'. We need to be quick. How long before Rose gets here?"

"It'll be about an hour and a half, they only left about forty minutes ago."

"Well, tell them to get their sirens going and get her picked up and back here pronto. Oh, and I want all the cars that are doing their rounds to look out for anything unusual. Did Rose tell you where she used to live?"

"Yes, they had a flat on Valley Road number 3b. He wouldn't still be living there, would he?"

"That's got to be where he's taken her. Sort out some backup and get the place surrounded. I'll meet you up there."

"Steve, don't go doing anything stupid. Wait until I get up there with backup before you go in." Nick said but he may as well have not wasted his breath, he knew Steve wasn't listening.

Steve arrived outside the block of flats. He couldn't wait for backup, he knew it wouldn't be long but he just couldn't wait. Emma might be in there fighting for her life. He unlocked the glove compartment of his car and pulled out his gun.

Steve entered the flats, they smelt of urine and the stairwell was gloomy. That's so typical, he thought, the lights aren't working. He walked up to the third floor, his eyes getting more accustomed to the dark as he ascended each stair.

Flat 3b. Steve knocked on the door. No answer. Steve knocked louder this time. Still no answer. "Open up police!" Steve shouted. Not a sound. A door opened just down the hall.

"What's going on?" Said a lady's voice.

"Police!" Steve said showing her his badge. "Please can you go back inside and lock your door. I'll let you know when it's safe to come out."

The door closed and was followed by the sound of a chain being pulled across.

"Come on Tony, I know you're in there. If you don't open up you know I'll just have to break the door down and I wouldn't want to make a mess of this tasteful residence."

"Detective Harris, how nice to hear your voice. On your own are you? I wouldn't break the door down if I were you. It would be a big, big mistake! You see I've got a knife at your girlfriend's pretty little throat." Tony suggested.

"Emma, are you ok?" Steve shouted frantically from outside the door to the flat.

"She's fine Detective Harris, for the moment anyway."

"Prove it! Let Emma speak."

"Let's prove to him that you still in the land of the living." Tony said pressing the knife just hard enough to pierce the skin on Emma's neck.

Emma squealed.

"What are you doing to her?"

"Oh Detective Harris you disappoint me. I can hear the panic in your voice. What happened to professional detective? Could it be that he's fallen in love? Are you in love with her? Is that why you haven't broken the door down already?" Tony sniggered.

Tony lent forward and licked the blood from Emma's neck. He groaned, taking pleasure in the fresh, warm blood.

"Get off me!" Emma screamed.

Steve was just about to break the door down when Nick came running up the stairs with two police officers in toe. "I thought I told you to wait for backup." He whispered.

"He's got her in there and he thinks that I'm on my own." Steve whispered.

"I feel it's time to surprise him then."

Steve and Nick slammed their bodies into the door. It only took two more times to bring the door down. Looking round the small living room Steve saw that the door to the bedroom was open.

Emma lay naked, all but a pair of knickers, on the bed, wrists and ankles tied to the bedposts. Tony was on top of her pressing a knife to her throat.

"Don't come any further or I'll kill her."

Steve pointed his gun at him. "Drop the knife Tony."

"I'm warning you, I'll kill her." Tony raised his knife in the air ready to plunge it down.

Steve aimed his gun and fired.

Chapter Twenty-Six

The bullet penetrated Tony's hand and he dropped the knife on the bed.

Steve rushed forward to get the knife but Tony grabbed it with his good hand and pushed it against the side of Emma's neck. Blood appeared from where the point of the knife had touched her neck, running down the side of her neck and onto the sheet. "Stay back Harris, she's mine!" Tony glared at him like a man possessed, eyes wild with fury at Harris for the searing pain that was now pulsating through his hand. "Just back the hell out of here and organize me a safe passage..."

Tony's demands were interrupted by blaring sirens and a screeching of tires as a car pulled up outside the building. Tony looked towards the large window with a door that led to the flat's balcony, which overlooked the street outside.

A sequential slamming of car doors was followed by a voice, "Tony! Tony can you hear me? It's Rosie, Tony! Your Rosie!"

Tony suddenly very puzzled, looked from Emma to the window and then from the window back to Emma.

"The girl you have in there isn't me Tony, she's called Emma not Rosie. I'm Rosie and I'm outside the window." The woman's voice pleaded.

"Go to the window." Steve said noticing Tony was in disbelief at what ears were telling him. "You'll see that it's Rosie outside, just go and look."

Stunned, Tony got off the bed and walked out of the bedroom and over to the window. Steve lowered his gun while Tony's back was turned and crept slowly over to where Emma lay. "You ok?" He whispered.

Emma nodded as he covered her with a blanket and started to untie her wrists and ankles. Steve looked at Nick Fisher and gave him a nod towards Tony who is now looking out the window, completely unaware of what is going on behind him.

Nick quietly creeps over to unarm and grab Tony before he realises and makes his move.

Suddenly Tony spots a reflective moment behind him in the window and turns shouting, "No!" Lifting the knife, he plunged it into Nick's chest and ripped it back out again as Nick fell to the floor in a crumpled heap. Tony ran like a man possessed at the bedroom where Steve was trying to untie Emma. Thinking on his feet, Steve grabbed his gun and shot Tony in the head. Tony slumped to the floor like a zombie taken out in a horror movie.

Epilogue

It was a cold but clear day as Jackie's coffin was lowered into the ground. The trees were bare, branches reaching up into the sky reminding Emma of the pictures you get in an anatomy book detailing the nervous system. Emma pulled her long black woollen coat tightly around her shoulders and approached the grave.

Dave was buried yesterday, and Jackie today, two funerals in as many days. Emma had lost two very good friends and there would be no justice for their deaths. No justice for the other girls that had been raped and murdered.

As Emma threw the red rose onto Jackie's coffin, a tear found its way from her eye down an imaginary path on her cheek. Her best friend's life was cut as short as the tear's life would be when it reached the bottom of her cheek, only to be soaked up by the collar of her coat.

Emma turned from the grave and walked over to Steve, who put a reassuring arm around her shoulders. Steve, who had only just buried his ex-wife last week, turned her to face him and said, "It's over now. It's all over." He pulled her into a tight hug.

Emma looked up at him and smiled weakly, "Is it really all over? It may be over for us but out there somewhere there always be another 'Tony'."